Nitro Mountain

Nitro Mountain

LEE CLAY JOHNSON

ALFRED A. KNOPF | NEW YORK | 2016

THIS IS A BORZOI BOOK
PUBLISHED BY ALFRED A. KNOPF

All rights reserved. Published in the United States by
Alfred A. Knopf, a division of Penguin Random House LLC,
New York, and in Canada by Random House of Canada,
a division of Penguin Random House Canada Limited, Toronto.

www.aaknopf.com

Knopf, Borzoi Books, and the colophon are registered
trademarks of Penguin Random House LLC.

Library of Congress Cataloging-in-Publication Data

Johnson, Lee Clay.
    Nitro Mountain / Lee Clay Johnson.—First edition.
        pages   cm
    ISBN 978-1-101-94636-7 (hardcover)—
ISBN 978-1-101-94637-4 (ebook)   1. Cities and
towns—Virginia—Fiction.   2. Country life—Virginia—
Fiction.   I. Title.
    PS3610.O3627N58   2016
    813'.6—dc23   2015027925

This is a work of fiction. Names, characters, places, and
incidents either are the product of the author's imagination
or are used fictitiously. Any resemblance to actual persons,
living or dead, events, or locales is entirely coincidental.

Jacket photograph by Raymond Gehman / National Geographic /
Getty Images
Jacket design by Oliver Munday

Manufactured in the United States of America
First Edition

To East Hundred

Nitro Mountain

1

We were sitting in my truck in front of the diner she was working at. Greg, her boss, had everybody convinced he was a genius.

"He's really smart," Jennifer said. "You know what he told me yesterday while I was in the kitchen?" I rolled down the window and let in cold air. She took face powder from the glove box, bent the rearview at her face and dusted her nose. Headlights came flickering from way behind us. "You don't even care," she said.

"I care," I said. "I'd like to kick his ass." The headlights were getting closer.

"Yeah, right. Remember when you found that wounded squirrel?"

I turned to see a lifted Tacoma with an aluminum hound cage in the bed rush past. Barks and bays twisted around us and then away as the taillights took the next turn.

"It was a baby. It was lost. It found me."

"You cried when it died."

"That was a while ago," I said.

"You've never even been hunting."

"I fish."

"Catch and release."

"I catch and keep, darling," I said, reaching for her jeans.

She knocked my hand away. Choosing not to hunt around here was tougher than doing it, given all the shit people talked if you weren't waddling around in orange come deer season. "Don't mess with Greg anymore," I said.

"Aw, look, it's jealous." She petted my arm.

Hand to chin, I pushed my head sideways, to the point of pain, and held it there until my neck cracked. She wasn't even going to kiss me. When things got like this between us, I had a habit of hurting myself in front of her. See if she'd say something.

She hummed to herself, checked her watch. "Don't be here when I get off," she said.

"How else you gonna get off?" I said.

"We're done. I'm leaving."

"Please," I said. "Don't."

She walked to the diner without looking back, smoothed a hand through her hair at the door and made sure she looked good before going in. She did. It was the end of November and the sun was barely cracking the sky. Clouds scattered above the northwest mountains. It got dark so early these days, and it never got all that light.

The town was shadowed by hills. One road this way, one road that way, and their unfortunate intersection was the main square with a brick courthouse that had seen nobler days. The Bordon post office, the library, empty storefronts and a couple shops that hadn't gone under yet. And then the abandoned Dairy Queen, my sister's apartment complex and this diner. North of town off 231, toward Nitro Mountain, were the gas station and the Foodville grocery store. Sprawl, if you could even call it that. Then the country opened up. My folks' place was out there. All the roads and houses seemed to be crushed beneath the foothills, on the verge of burial. West of everything, mountains scraped the sky. At night you could see a red light on top of Nitro Mountain.

South of town was a tiny church with a homeless shelter in the basement. I worked there part-time for cash, morning shifts that involved standing behind a desk only a foot away from so many crises worse than mine, or just running around and handing out towels and soap. It was a strange thing for me to be doing. I always felt closer to the other side of the desk.

On a morning when I'd shown up to help open the shelter after a night of playing bluegrass music and drinking blended whiskey, one of the old bums stepped to the desk to sign in, gazed through my skull, grinned and said, "You look worse than I do today. And I'm a dead man walking." He looked around. "Somebody do math?"

When things slowed down that day I grabbed a single-size bottle of mouthwash from the dental drawer and jogged upstairs to the employee bathroom. A few sticky blinks. The room rocked. I swished the shot of Scope and before spitting I checked the label for the alcohol percentage. Hard to read. Looked high. Not that bad. I swallowed and it made me feel better, and for that I felt worse.

Since then, I had promised myself never to stay out late before a morning shift. No matter what. Even if I was playing music. Even if the drinks were free. Even if my girlfriend had just left me. And there was the problem: I had a shift tomorrow morning at six and my girlfriend just left me. I needed to go get one drink and figure out what the hell had just happened to my life. I wouldn't be able to sleep if I didn't.

The last time I'd been seriously drunk with Jennifer, she wanted to fight so bad that when I didn't raise a hand she hit herself right in front of me. I begged her to quit as she threw her fist into her face over and over again, then said, "You coward, if you won't do it, somebody's got to."

We were guilty of the same strange cruelties, hurting ourselves to hurt the other, then crawling back and asking forgiveness. She often said I was too soft, and out of everything she called me, that hurt the most because it was true.

I drove to Durty Misty's, a bar on the edge of town where I

sometimes backed up country bands on bass. It was a good spot to get shitty, and while driving over there I decided that's what I was going to do tonight.

The place was almost empty when I walked in. I'd never come here just to drink. It was always with a band on a busy night. One guy sat at the end of the bar playing Nudie Photo Hunt. A picture of a woman in a small torn bikini appeared on the screen and then broke apart into little squares. He pieced her back together before his time ran out, otherwise he would've lost her.

I sat down and told the bartender I wanted something that would make me hard. He was a quiet guy who looked at me like he couldn't hear a thing I said.

"Give the boy what I'm drinking," the man playing Photo Hunt said. He turned away from the game. There was a Daffy Duck tattoo on the side of his neck and I recognized him from the shelter. He showed up every now and then, never to eat, never to do laundry or to get help printing a résumé. Just to look around, take a few books from the free library and leave. The books he took were often classics. Lots of tattered Greek tragedies. The occasional Charlotte Lamb romance. He didn't know who I was and I didn't bring it up.

"Thanks," I said.

"Try shutting your mouth more while you're talking." He picked his tooth with the snapped prong of a plastic fork, shook his head. "Somebody do something," he said. "Now."

The bartender poured whiskey, beer and pickled jalapeño brine into a blue mason jar. He mixed it with a soda straw, placed the jar in front of me and then backed it with a tiny birdbath of bourbon in the jar's upturned lid.

"Drink half the drink," the man said. "Then shoot the shot. And then." He paused and considered the wall of bottles behind the bar. His pinkie and thumb winged out from his hand while three ringed fingers rubbed the tattoo into his throat. A small airplane made of beer cans hung from the ceiling on fishing line.

"And then drink the rest of it?" I said.

"No. And then fuck the rest of it." He turned to the bartender, sucked his fingers and tapped the bone between his eyebrows. It sounded like wet wood. "Who is this sitting next to me, Bob?"

"I dunno."

"Has he been here before?" He pressed the tattoo like he was taking his pulse.

"Yeah."

"How do you know?"

"I dunno."

Bob was right. I had been here many times, but I was always hiding behind my bass at the back of the band.

"Does he know what we do?"

"Probably not."

"What do you know? Do you know shit? Tell me what you do know, Old Bob."

"You want another drink," Bob said. He had the eyes of a boy, and orange cracker crumbs at the sides of his mouth. His hair was caught up in a bad Elvis situation. Paper clips held some of it together.

The man stood up and started clapping. "Thank God! Hallelujah! Fuck it. You know a lot more than we give you credit for. Ladies and gentlemen," he announced to the empty room, "please give Bob the bartender a hand. He knows every fucking thing."

Bob took a bow. Some of his comb-over fell forward as he went down, and when he came up a length remained standing.

The man quit clapping and ordered himself another one of what I was drinking. "Hell yes, heaven time," he said, and drained the shot. He moved the other drink to and from his mouth with both hands, like he was operating some big machine, and then looked straight between Bob and me and asked, "You know why a girl's got two holes?"

I didn't, and neither did Bob.

"So you can carry her around like a six-pack."

Bob started fixing his hair.

The man looked intent, like he'd just imparted some essential information. "Get it?" he said. "Do you get it?" Past the plane, a clock was nailed into the wall. It wasn't even nine yet. Or maybe it was.

I don't know how I made it back to the diner, don't even remember driving, but that's where I landed when I stepped out of the cab just in time to see the building's lights going out. Chairs were upside down on tables and I could see all their legs in the air, a hundred little whores taking it. Drinks had worked and I was drunk. I leaned against the hood and the heat of the engine warmed my jacket sleeve. The stars were so bright the sky looked like the diner's speckled countertop.

A door shut in the back of the building. I tripped, steadied myself. Walking could not be beyond me.

The front of the diner was a retro singlewide. The kitchen and the dish room were in a cinderblock addition stuck behind it. I found Jennifer and Greg standing back there together near the dumpster. He had a full trash bag on the ground beside him, and when he saw me he said, "Who the hell's that?"

"That's him," Jennifer whispered.

"What'd you just call me?" I said.

"'Him'?" she said.

"I ain't going anywhere without you."

"Oh, boy. This kind of thing?" Greg lifted the trash bag and carried it to the bin. A broken bottle cut through the black plastic and caught the light of the security lamp. When he turned around I was on him, asking how he liked me now, and I swung on him. Things went spinning and I fell against the dumpster and slid down into a sitting position.

"That's embarrassing," he said, and kicked me in the side. Air left my lungs like a puncture. I couldn't stand up, couldn't say anything, couldn't think. I should've asked if that was all he had, but I just kept looking at Jennifer.

"Let's get out of here," she said, tugging at him. "C'mon. Before he gets himself up."

"We can't just leave him here."

"Teach him a lesson," she said.

While they were walking back to his car, she turned around to look at me. There wasn't pity in her face anymore. I saw approval. I was exactly what she wanted—someone to leave again. Maybe for good this time.

We weren't living together or anything like that, and honestly, if you'd asked her whether we were a couple, she would've said no. I was crazy for her because she wasn't crazy for me. I could see that now. The first time we met was so wonderful it made me believe she'd said things she never said. It was during a gig. I was onstage and she was the only one dancing. She kept her eyes on me. After, we made out against somebody's car. She said we'd never part. She said she wanted to be with me the rest of her life. Without even moving her mouth. We didn't spend the night together, just fell down right there on the concrete. The months following, I drove her around places, helped her get little things done, took her to various jobs. Never asked for gas money. The skin under her shirt was untouched, almost translucent, and I could not, no matter how hard I tried, let that go.

Tires shot gravel and she and Greg sped south down 231. I made it back to my truck and picked my keys up off the floorboard.

I should've seen it coming back when I was the one driving her around. I'd roll over to her apartment, this single-room efficiency thing with a raw mattress lying crooked in the middle of the floor, and just walk in without knocking. Once I found her curled up on the mattress beneath a mess of sheets and shirts and jeans. Everything smelled of her body and I knelt beside her and breathed it all in. "You," I said. "You're gonna be late."

"I quit."

"Since when?"

"Since just now." She'd been working for some photographer, doing what she said he called "tasteful erotic web work." He was paying her to be what she was—gorgeous—and though I'd been hoping she'd quit, I didn't get why she'd chosen this morning to do it.

"Is it 'cause I told you to?"

She snarled, clawed the air and kicked off the clothing and sheets. "Them motherfuckers don't own me." She sat up. "And neither do you. Let's go take me for a ride."

I leaned in for her lips, but she pressed two fingers against my forehead and pushed me back to where I'd been sitting.

"You're like, panting?" she said.

"I can't help it."

She pulled her hair back, slid a rubber band off her wrist. "So unique!" she said. "A guy that can't help it. Who'd've guessed?"

"What's that supposed to mean?"

"Can I just say something?"

"I'm sure you can."

She tied her hair up and pushed it back. The way her breasts hung there with her elbows raised like that—I had to look away, else I'd have lost control.

"Go start your truck," she said. "I'll be right out."

"I left it running."

"Well," she said. "Get out there, turn it off and then start it up again."

We took 231, the same stretch down which I was now chasing her and Greg, but things were different back then; new leaves were out on the trees, bright as katydids. We popped open the vent-windows and the warm air came blowing onto our laps and flowing through the cab. We shared every cigarette we smoked and we must've gone through half a pack before she said, "So. You asked me what I meant. A man that can't help himself. You ready for this?"

I said yes but knew I wasn't.

She talked for a while, building it up big, said when she was twelve she used to smoke weed in her friend's basement. She'd light up under the stairs hoping maybe God wouldn't notice, but she finally decided God probably had the ability—who knows how or why He even gives a crap—to see her most secret things, and even though she hated Him for this she came to terms with her sins. The only time in her life she believed God really cared about her was the day she went down there to smoke and found a present wrapped up under the stairs with her name on it. That filled her with a joy she couldn't describe. She opened it and there, folded inside, lay a pair of blue socks. The note on top of them said *From Good Steve.*

"You don't know who that is," she said. "Good Steve was my friend's dad and it was his house. He'd never given me nothing before except kisses when I slept over."

"Kisses?" I said.

"Just little pop-kiss things. That and the time he taught me how to give him a blow job."

"The fuck?" I hated hearing that there'd been anybody other than me.

"It happened in his daughter's room, my friend, who I'm not

going to say her name. It was in her bedroom and I was on the trundle bed. She was off taking a bath or something."

"Jesus, Jenn. Was he touching her too?"

"No way. Just me. That's how it's always been. Look at me. I was pretty much the same when I was twelve as I am now. Just more pure. Not as busted. Can you imagine? You would've loved it. No other girls got the attention I got. It was because of how I looked. It wasn't about him at all. I took it as a compliment. Still do. I remember giggling with it in my mouth. I didn't know what else to do with it. He couldn't help himself, you know?"

I kicked the gas and the truck swerved.

"I was just a little girl. I wouldn't hang out with anybody like him anymore. Well, maybe not." She poked me. "But I did have a crush on him. He wasn't a predator. I kind of asked for it."

"No you didn't."

"It split my lips when he was putting it in."

"I'm sorry to hear that." I didn't know if she was fucking with me or not. She was shaking her words like they were on a string held between her teeth.

"The next day it was like I had canker sores. You like how that sounds?"

The steering wheel was slick in my hands. I kept my eyes on the road. The world outside was flying by in a blur. There was a turn ahead I knew I couldn't make at this speed.

"In the basement the day I got my present," she said, "I put my feet into those socks and they fit perfect. How did Good Steve know? I never had socks so nice. I promised myself I would never forget them anywhere. I promised to always keep them. Forever. It looked like a mother's hands had made them. And maybe so. Maybe my friend's mother, Good Steve's wife. I'm wearing them right now. Wanna see?"

She pulled her pant leg up and flashed one of the socks. Then she vanished. I couldn't make the turn. Daylight broke apart into pieces of shattering glass. I was alone and it was a dark night out, and freezing cold, and she wasn't there anymore and I couldn't protect her.

"Oscar, you are amazing graces." My sister's face against a hospital ceiling.

"What's wrong?" I said. "Why you here, Krystal?"

But soon I realized it was me she was worried about, me why she was here and me why I was here. A cast held my arm in place, and when I tried to move it a shock of light flashed behind my eyes. I only remembered taillights I couldn't catch.

She told me the truck flipped and landed on its side. The cops found me stuck there in my seat belt. When they looked into my window, I'd said, "Nothing to see here, ociffer." It was all written down in the report. Apparently there were recordings of it that I was welcome to listen to. I had broken my arm and totaled my truck. The hospital released me later that day, and Krystal drove me to the station down a strip littered with stores like Virginia Cash Cow, Tony's Terrific Title Loans and a couple doc-in-a-box places. One of them, the Med Care Clinic, was where my mom worked. At the station I picked up some of my things and learned I was being charged with a DUI, reckless driving, damage of public and private property, plus some other shit I couldn't afford. I would've been in the drunk tank, but the hospital had been the first stop and my injuries were bad enough that they just let me stay. Everybody was nice about everything. They didn't even allow me the luxury of feeling like a mean guy.

Krystal waited on a bench on the sidewalk, and when I came out she stood up and asked if I was done, like I'd been shopping. I hadn't accomplished shit in my life, and it was embarrassing to have her here for this milestone.

"I'm done," I said. "Done for good."

"Oh, Oscar," she said. She called me Oscar because the only thing I'd ever liked on *Sesame Street* was the Grouch. We'd spent a portion of our young lives in foster care, before a couple from the church took us in and fed us saltines and juice and let us play with their yellow Lab for a couple years, then we moved back in with our parents after my mom had finally shown the courts she could keep our lives together. There was nothing interesting about any of it. At the beginning of ninth grade I was expelled for reasons that aren't even worth explaining. I spent the next ten years hanging around town, between my sister's apartment and my parents' house, sometimes living with a friend for a while until he told me I needed to start pulling my own weight, which I could never do.

"You still have a lot ahead of you," she said.

"That's what I'm afraid of."

"I like when you smile," she said. Her eyes were the color of lake ice. Her hair was blond, mine mud brown. I wondered if we came from different people.

"I'm not smiling," I said. "My arm hurts."

"It reminds me of Grandpa. Y'all were so much alike. I wish you could've known him at an older age."

Grandpa had been a motorcycle-riding military man turned whiskey-drinking minister. He would disappear late every week and show up at his Sunday morning services smelling of it. Communion, for him, was hair of the dog. Everybody said he swore off the stuff later in life, but the damage had been done and he had maintained a haze of drunkenness in everything he did— broad gestures and a loud voice for minor occasions. At family picnics he'd make trips to the trunk to check on the spare tire, the one thing I did remember. His great tragedy, my sister liked to say, was that he couldn't express the love he felt for me.

"Boo-hoo for him," I always said back.

My truck had been his before he died. He gave it to Krystal

and she gave it to me, telling me to keep the oil changed, which was the first thing I didn't do.

Let me say something about that truck. It was a 1980 F-150 Ranger Explorer V8 longbed with double gas tanks and an aluminum brush guard on the grille. The paint job was the color of autumn. The bench seat was the size of a sofa, like you were rolling down the road in your living room. You could sleep in the cab if you had to, and more than once I did. But those are other stories, and what hurt now was this: The one thing my grandfather had given us to show his love, I had thrown away. What did that make me?

My sister asked where I wanted to go. None of my friends were talking to me, so I told her our parents'. I hated saying it, but with my wheels gone, my arm broke and no money, I was going to need a place to sit down and figure shit out.

Krystal offered her place, but I could hear hesitation in her voice. I'd been there the last few nights. Who wants to live with their loser little brother? Who wants to see him become everything you overcame?

The first week wasn't so bad. Mom worked daylong shifts at Med Care and would come home at odd hours in the evening not wearing her work clothes. Dad stayed in bed with back problems, waiting for his disability. He got stoned in the mornings and kept quiet until lunch. I'd bring him a sandwich and a couple cracked cans of Bud. Sometimes he'd send me over to the neighbors' house, a family by the name of Habitte, to buy more pot from Nicholas, their high school son. My room hadn't changed at all, still a couple sunken mattresses and that same rat-matted carpet underneath everything.

My Fender P Bass leaned against the wall in the corner,

plugged into a Peavey practice amp. It was nice to see it there. I ran my finger along its body through the dust and drew a line of gloss across the top horn.

It was the left arm I'd broken, and my cast kept the elbow bent at such an angle that when I flipped the on switch on, sat down and put the bass in my lap, I was pretty much ready to play. I tuned it up. There was a cassette player on top of the TV that still had a practice tape in it. Mostly country and blues and rock. Loud, overstated bar stuff. I played along until my arm sizzled and sent glowing lines of pain up my wrist and into my backbone. Waiting for things to ease, I went for a walk behind the house to make sure my legs still worked.

We lived against a forest of cedar and pine that peaked to a point of beech trees the color of bone. The other side of the hill sloped down into maples, oaks and hickory. I wandered along the fence line and watched the sun toss flakes of gold into the sky. The pain in my arm and side had faded. A pack of hounds in the distance. I worried that my life had ended, and then that it hadn't.

The reason I decided to play the bass was because I'd heard everybody was always looking for bass players. Apparently that had changed. There was even a cover band in town that admitted they didn't have a bass, and said no, they didn't want one.

I called the shelter and asked if they needed anyone to cover shifts. They asked where I'd been, and why I'd missed my last few mornings. When I told them, they said, "Okay. We've been worried. Don't come back."

"But I need you," I said.

"We're open every day," the lady said. "You're welcome here to wash your clothes, take a shower, eat a meal." Her name was

Alisha. I'd heard her use her phone voice before, but I never thought it would be directed at me.

Mom was starting to get on my case about the electricity I was pulling in my room, and I kept promising her I'd figure something out. One cold Saturday I took a one-handed bike ride over to Durty Misty's. I had bassman-for-hire flyers in my backpack. The only thing between our house and the bar was the Foodville and the Joy Imperial gas station. I wobbled into the parking lot there to tape a flyer up in their window.

Somebody must've been watching me, because when I set my bike against the front wall the door opened for a couple seconds, bells swinging from the inside handle. I followed a woman to the counter. Little jewels and studs stuck into the ass of her jeans. She turned around and I recognized her face from high school. "Rachel?" I said.

"It's you," she said. "You! Um. What's your name again?"

"It's Leon."

"I'm sorry, I'm sorry. I knew that."

"But you didn't."

The smell of burning dust on the space heater in the corner filled the room. She sat behind the register. "So this is how you reignite old friendships?" she said. "You kick it off by getting pissed about something?"

"I'm just. I don't know. It's been." I motioned to my cast.

"I see that," she said. "What happened?"

"Nothing. I saved a bunch of people's lives. Not worth talking about right now. It's all in the past. Well, okay, not really the past. But, you know, nothing important."

Coolers lined the walls of the small room, enclosing shelves of bagged chips and a maze of candy racks. She shook her head and threw a strand of hair out of her face. "What's wrong with you?" she said.

"Look, I got some flyers here. I need work. Hey, I saw the sign out there. Y'all're hiring?"

"You don't want to work here," she said.

"It's not about wanting to."

"They pay me to sit here and push buttons. What are the flyers for?"

"I can push buttons."

"They're paying minimum wage." She sat back down and pulled at her breast pocket. "Anyway," she said, catching my eyes on her chest, "you'd be distracted."

"Maybe you're right." I went to leave.

"Wait," she said. "Aren't you going to ask me out?"

"Will you say yes?"

"Maybe."

"Rachel," I said.

I pushed the door open with my foot, making the bells bang around, and she said, "We're not allowed to put up flyers anymore. It's like the lost dog capital of the world around here."

"They're flyers for me. Bass player looking for band."

"So you're the lost dog," she said. "Try Misty's."

It was too early for them to be open when I got there, but I knocked on the door a few times anyway. The black-painted metal had a peephole in the middle. I didn't knock again. From my backpack I took a flyer and looked for a spot on the wall where all the rain-stained show posters hung. I slapped my advertisement up and pinned it in there, then walked away and turned around to see how it looked. But I kept noticing the peephole—bright, and then dark, and then bright again, like the door was winking.

The next Friday, everybody but me was out partying. I was in the kitchen doing dishes, scrubbing taco beef off plates. My cast was still on and I had trouble holding things while I scrubbed them with my good hand. I didn't bother with much rinsing, just stacked them with suds sliding down all over. The doorbell rang and from the couch Mom called, "Come in, come in, whoever you are." She was feeling good because I was finally doing something.

I knew who it was the minute he cleared his throat. Jones Young. Guitar player and singer. He wasn't a lot older than me but he came across as an elder. A big deal in the bluegrass and old school country scene. He was respected by purists who wouldn't give me the time of day; I was just some overgrown kid playing loud music for girls. Jones knew all the standards and was a great rhythm player. Fiddlers liked him because he kept good time and rarely took solos. Banjo players liked him because he always brought the booze. One of the things that made him different from everybody else was that he liked me.

He also wrote his own songs, stuff that actually made you think. When he wanted to get rowdy, he'd put an outlaw country-rock band together that he called Jones & the Young Divorcés. That band was how we knew each other. He used me for bass. It was also how I met Jennifer.

I peeked into the living room and saw him standing there. He held a smoking cigarette toward our storm door like it hadn't closed behind him. "Missus Carol," he was saying, laying it on thick. "I haven't seen you in a while. How ever are you? You look wonderful. By any chance is Leon around?"

"Oh, he's in there," she said, "busy acting busy."

"How you, Jones?" I said, wiping my hand across the lap of my pants.

"Whoa, dude. What the hell happened to your arm?"

"You should see the other guy," I said.

Mom sang a word: "Buhuhullsheeeeit."

Jones shook his head and laughed, blowing smoke out his nose. He wore a denim jacket over a pearl-snap shirt tucked into worn-out jeans. Polished cowboy boots. "Damn," he said. "I was gonna ask you—"

"It still works," I said. "See?" I played some air bass for him.

Mom told him I'd been practicing along to the tape. "You wouldn't believe it," she said.

"What? That he's practicing?"

"Thing is," I said, "I've only got that little amp."

"Good," he said. "You can use it as a monitor. It's got a direct out, right? We can mic it and run it through the house mains." The show was tonight, his regular bassist had backed out after double-booking and we were on in an hour. "If you don't mind me taking your dishwasher," Jones said to my mom.

"They'll still be dirty when he gets back."

I ran to my room, holding my arm to make sure I didn't knock it against anything.

I'd barely gotten the bass strap over my shoulder when the drummer clicked us into "Always Late." I stumbled my way behind them up to the 4, this stupid little two-hit they liked to do, and as soon as I dropped back into the 1, I found the pocket and for the first time in a long while I knew what I was meant to be doing.

It didn't feel like my arm was broken at all. I moved around the fingerboard like I was healed, and maybe I was, just for now. The place was packed and people were dancing. I looked to Jerry, the drummer, his arms crossed as he held a tight shuffle on the high hat and snare, his head pointing upward with his mouth open like he was trying to catch a stream of fresh water falling from the sky. I looked to Matt, the lead guitarist, thrusting into the back of his Telecaster when he bent strings. Jones was turned to us with his ear to the floor, checking to hear if the engine we'd cranked up was firing on all cylinders.

One country standard after another. Those songs, that music—when it's done right it plays itself.

We were halfway into the first set when I saw Rachel. She had her arms in the air, a beer in one hand, and was dancing around with her eyes closed like she was climbing an invisible ladder. All kinds of bad dudes were looking at her. Nobody was talking to her. Then the man with the Daffy Duck tattoo handed her another drink.

When the set break came, Jerry pulled a pack of Camels from his cymbal case, said it wasn't his fault and stepped off the stage.

"Who?" I said.

"It's your first gig with us in a while," Jones said. "You're doing fine. For the first one."

"If he'd just waited for me," I said of Jerry.

"Jerry always does that. Don't take it personal. He thinks it's fun, throwing everybody off." Jones thumbed toward the audience. "Anyway. I think you already got *one* fan."

People were talking and laughing as classic rock came on through the busted house speakers. She sat on a stool with her back to the bar, staring at me. I bent down to pick up a cord, pretending I hadn't noticed her, but when I'd gotten everything situated our eyes met and she motioned for me to come over.

I carried a tallboy in my cast hand. The crowd was thinning from people going outside to smoke and take nips from bottles hidden in their trucks. She had thin, painted lips and drawn cheeks like she was permanently sucking on something. She looked like a different person, wearing so much makeup. This could happen.

"So your flyer must've worked," she said, taking her feet off the stool's footrest, her legs stretching straight to the floor while she stayed sitting. She turned a can vertical to her mouth, crushed the middle with her fingers when she was through and set it behind her on the bar. Bob replaced it with a cold one.

"I've played with these boys before," I said. "That was only like a week or two ago I put up the flyer here. That day we saw each other."

"Only? How long you expect you got left?"

"Until what?"

"Till you run out of chances." She reached behind her without looking and grabbed the fresh beer. "You didn't even get my number."

The man with the Daffy Duck tattoo was standing too close to us. He kept grabbing his belt buckle and shaking it. "Feel good," he said, nodding in agreement with himself. "I feel all right. Swell. Decent. Indecent exposure. I feel fucking fantastic. I like good music. I'm a man of pure taste."

"I'll be right back." She walked around the stage and into the pinball room.

"She going to use the little girls' room," he said. "Come here."

I followed him into the back room where they made sandwiches. It reeked of rancid sliced meats and warm mayo. A door ajar in the corner and roaches racing across the floor. He pulled the chain of a bare lightbulb above us and we were in a cleaning-supply closet. He reached around me and shut the door.

We stood shoulder to shoulder among gallons of Clorox, rags and buckets, mops and brooms. He took an iPhone out of his pocket and set it upright on a shelf. He flicked his fingers across the screen, tapped a code into the keypad and told me to watch. He pulled the chain and the light went out. A dim image appeared on the screen. The glow of the phone transformed his face into that of a corpse, skull bones pushing through skin.

"Look at me," he said. He was breathing harder. Our eyes met for the first time and he said, "Watch me watch this."

"Thanks," I said, "but I better get back onstage."

"You'll never make it." He held out his hands as if offering some great revelation.

"I won't?"

"I'm seeing your future right now. It's not there." He got a small plastic bag out of his pocket, took a rock from it and packed it into a glass pipe. "No harm done," he said. "We're just two extremely nice gentlemen." The lighter flicked and he took a hit. "Any minute," he said, holding his breath and turning back to the screen. "Done no harm." The smoke he blew into the room smelled like burnt mints. "My brother," he said, "be not afraid."

I leaned over to see what he was watching, and he grabbed my cast.

"Watch *me*," he said.

In the glow of his phone he licked his dry lips. The door opened and the glare of the sandwich room came in. The crowd was loud out at the bar. Jerry kicked his bass drum a couple times, my cue. Old Bob stood there in the doorway and whined like a puppy.

"Shut the door," the man said, "shut the door, shut the fucking door."

Bob pushed past me and held out a kind of pencil, presenting it to us like it was some secret key.

"Draw it," the man said. "It's about to happen. Draw it."

Bob turned the pencil toward his own face and started drawing lines around his eyes. Broken circles of black eyeliner traced the inside of his sunken sockets and zagged onto his face. The man took another hit from his pipe, moaning and begging for something, I couldn't tell what, and then turned back to the screen. "It's happening," he said, stuffing a fist down his Dickies.

Black streaks ran down Bob's cheeks. He was crying. The man passed him the pipe without turning away from the phone and Bob grabbed at it, pulling hard when the flame finally found the little rock, then exhaled and touched his fingers on the Daffy Duck.

I glanced between them at what they were watching. A white border circled the screen but something else was emerging in the middle of the frame. I leaned closer and the man roared into my face, took his fist from his pants and punched me in the stomach. "Have y'all been doing druggies?"

"Oh, no!" Bob said, then splayed his fingers over his sketched eyes, opened them enough to peek through and said, "Oh, no no no!"

I heard Jerry kick his bass drum again.

"That's my cue," I said.

"Your cue," the man said. "What if somebody just stepped into your life one day and *took* your cue?" Tears were soaking into the cracked skin of his cheekbones, but it didn't seem like crying. He looked dizzy. "What if they took it out from under you like a rug and you realized there was no floor under you."

"I don't know what you're saying." But what he said made me wonder. What if I didn't have any excuses? What if, like Rachel had said, I was running out of chances?

"Go fetch your cue," the man said. "But don't tell Mommy or nobody y'all been doing druggies." He inhaled again and Bob pushed my head into the man's face. Our lips found each other's and he blew smoke into my mouth.

The two erupted into something that wasn't laughter. I made it back into the packed barroom and pushed toward the stage, looking for Rachel with every shove. I picked up my bass and saw her coming out of the pinball room. Customers were going behind the bar and pulling their own drafts, tossing nickels into the tip jar. Bob came out with a dark mess smeared around his eyes.

Jones stomped a pedal tuner and turned around to face me. "The hell were you doing in there?"

"Where? Oh—they just wanted to hang out."

"Stay away from those dudes. Especially if you're playing with me. You hear? I won't have it."

"Yeah," I said, "no problem."

It felt like flying, talking to Jones and feeling the stuff start to kick. I had something nobody else could touch.

Jones went back to the mic, stomped the pedal again and counted us in. The music was even better now, the pocket deep and the melody soaring. Jones's voice sounded so close through the system that I could picture his vocal cords, long and rough. I was floating above the crowd now, but Jerry snapped the snare to bring me back down and he yelled at me over the music to get my shit together. But whatever cloud the man had blown into my mouth was beautiful, and I'd never felt sharper in all my life.

After the gig, I sat at one of the tables out on what people were calling the veranda, these pieces of plywood nailed onto pallets in the parking lot with red Christmas lights strung from garden posts Quikreted into the cracked asphalt. Rachel was hovering around me, talking to a few straggling regulars, and I was listening for one of them to say her name, to see how well she knew them. That's how I planned on trusting her.

The band had left with the tip bucket, and for pay I was stuck drinking pints of Natty Light, which really wasn't so bad. She'd already offered to drive me home but I still didn't want to go. One more beer? Why not. Bob had tried to rub away the eyeliner and by now he just looked dirty. He stood at my table, arms behind his back like he was trying to undo his own bra, asking if I wanted a new beverage.

"Another one of these," I said.

"Another those," he said, and sidestepped over to Rachel, who was now talking to a group of guys about how hard it was to be a woman. "It's like," she said. "It's like," she said. "It's like."

They nodded along with her, following her point: It *is* like.

"Order now or forever hold your peas," Bob said, cupping his crotch.

One guy smacked his hand away and asked for a round of whiskeys.

"How round?" Bob said, reaching for Rachel's breasts.

"Do it," she said, "and I'll bite your nose off."

"It's all right, Rachel," another guy said. "He don't mean nothing by it."

When I went back in to pack my gear, I did something on purpose.

After I'd slid my bass into its bag, I left my power cord and guitar cable on the corner of the stage. Daffy Duck was mopping up behind the bar, sweating and cursing at himself. I expected him to look over as I walked by, but he didn't. With the gig bag over my right shoulder, the amp in that hand and my broken arm thumping hot pain through my neck, I kicked open the door and dumped it out on the edge of the veranda. The shots the group ordered had come out, and Rachel left the circle to hand me mine. "Here's to you," she said. "For trying."

I wasn't sure what she meant. Trying to play bass? Trying to get with her? Trying to be a big boy and carry my own shit? But I tapped my shot glass against hers, splashing a burning drizzle of whiskey over the hangnail on my thumb.

Daffy led Bob, who was crying again, in by the shirt collar, and without looking at me Rachel said she wanted to go.

"I'm riding with you," I said.

"I'll load your stuff," she said. "It looks heavy. Don't lift a thing. You looked all night like you were hurting."

She had a green Subaru Outback with one blue door. "A train hit me one time," she said. "It was going five miles an hour."

"Story of my life," I said.

She fit my stuff in the back among jugs of antifreeze, oil, transmission fluid. The heat in her car was a miracle; it even came up out of the leather seats. I told her to drive slow so we could enjoy it.

She lived in a condo on top of a treeless yard. A basketball goal lay on its side across part of the driveway with sand pouring out of its base. "The family that lived in the other half of the house left it like that," she said. "A Mexican bunch that was always fixing my car for free. They moved out last week. We can stretch our limbs tonight. Make all the noise we want."

We were walking up the stairs to her front door when the blinds in the picture window broke open, then snapped shut. I stopped at the top step and asked who was in there.

"Why so nervous?"

I wanted to tell her that I was fine with coming inside tonight, especially since I needed a place to stay. I would do it as long as I didn't have to get to know her. It was about Jennifer. "Is somebody else here?" I said.

"It's just my dog. He crashes the blinds when he gets excited. Nobody ever comes over. Until they do."

I slept soundly for the first time since Jennifer had ditched me. Rachel's boxer was there on the bed where she'd been, twisting on its back, all muscle and muzzle, snorting and sneezing. The smell of bacon came into the room in the dog's coat and made me think of my folks' place. I should've told them I wasn't coming home. But I was old enough. I didn't have to call anybody.

Rachel bounded onto the bed with the dog and they both covered me in kisses and paws and fingers, like we were actually lovers.

"Food's almost done," she said. "Come on." She kissed my cheek and stood up over me, her nylon nightgown opening, and on the lower cheek of her ass I saw a tattoo of lips, three little words printed under it.

"That," I said, and touched it.

"Kiss my ass."

"Let me."

She stepped off the bed and said, "I gotta," holding herself. The thought of her going in there to do that sent a rush through my groin, but I slid into my jeans and walked down the hallway to the kitchen, slowing past the bathroom to hear her pissing.

Over eggs and bacon I told her, "They're up to some bullshit at Misty's."

"I didn't know you were a detective."

"No. I mean, really." The black coffee steamed in her bright kitchen. By the time we'd finished talking about Misty's, what I'd seen, it was cold and untouched. "Drive me over there and I'll prove it," I said.

"Don't you think it's best to sometimes let things be?"

"Sometimes, yeah. I just got to pick up a couple cords."

"If you'll leave it at that. I don't want to get involved in this nonsense."

"You might already be."

"They're not even open yet," she said. "Not for another few hours."

"Hey," I said, getting an idea. I threw the coffee back, took her to the bedroom and kicked the dog out.

The day was the kind of clean and clear that almost made the weather seem warm. The top branches of a twisting white oak caught the light as we turned onto the road to town. The bare mountainside was the color of a deer. She clicked the radio to some station playing opera. I never liked that music, didn't understand it, but this time a man's voice wailed out an endless lonesome cry, and I knew exactly what he was saying. He was just some lost dude, down on his luck and looking for love. All he had to his name was a busted heart. And that's all he needed. I turned the volume up, closed my eyes and listened.

She parked in front of the veranda, the front tires butting against a pallet.

"Careful," I said.

"*You* be careful."

The pub door sucked shut behind me. Pine walls slick and blackened, a low dropped ceiling with fluorescent lights. "Anybody here?" I called toward the kitchen. "Just getting my shit."

Next to the cash register Bob's front half lay stretched across the bar. His head rested on a folded arm while the other reached out in front of him, as if ready to take payment. The greased hairdo flopped over dead. His dentures had slid halfway out of his mouth. I walked past him and gathered my cords. Didn't take but a second, and then I slid back to the pinball machines, past buzzers and flashing lights and into the ladies' room and the sharp stink of urine and bleach.

A little black thing like a clip-on microphone was stuck outside the toilet up around the back of the bowl with a kind of lens that looked like a water droplet. A thin black cable snuck down to the floor and into the wall. In case somebody was watching, I grabbed some toilet paper so I'd have an excuse and took it to the men's room. I stood around for an ass-wiping minute and then stepped out like nothing was wrong, just a bass player come to get his usual forgottens.

Bob was where I'd left him, but now he was on his other side, the mirror image of a minute ago. The heater hanging from the ceiling coughed a blast of dry air into my hair and poured out rolling fumes of oil heat.

When I got back outside, I gasped as if I'd been holding my breath the whole time. The man with the tattoo was leaning against Rachel's car. "You," he said. "What's everybody call you?" He was staring at the ground beside me.

I lifted the cables in my good hand to show him why I'd been in there, but then I saw what I still held in my left hand: the roll of toilet paper.

He looked at my face. "Now I'm interested," he said.

"Oh," I said. "Nothing."

"Really?" He walked up and, without taking his eyes from mine, grabbed the toilet paper. "Because that looks like my double ply."

Back in the car, Rachel and I kept quiet. It seemed darker even though there were still no clouds. Or maybe there was just one big one that had slugged in to cover everything.

"Well, that was weird as hell back there," she said.

"What'd he say to you?"

"Nothing, really. I'm talking about what you did. The toilet paper."

"How well do you know him?"

"Met him the other night," she said. "First time. Swear."

"You know what's going on at that place?"

"Those guys are weirdos, straight up. But I think you're making a big deal out of nothing."

"Let me tell you what I saw."

"But I won't believe you, right?"

"You decide," I said, and then told her about the little thing on the toilet bowl, that guy in the closet with his iPhone. "They were watching. Or whatever. Somebody ought to call the cops on him."

"Then where would you play? Where would we drink?"

I thought about that. She had her points. "It's just nasty," I said. "What he's doing in there, it's wrong."

"Somebody bring in the string section. Why you think he asked *you* into the closet? He probably thought you came off as the kind of guy who'd like that sort of thing."

"Well, I'm not."

"You sure about that?"

After we went back to her place to pick up my bag, I asked her to drop me off at my sister's. Krystal lived in a white-and-tan apartment complex called River Creek. The name gave me a headache. Why not just call it Alive Dead? When Rachel pulled away, before I'd made it up onto the sidewalk, she blew me a kiss without looking.

I heard talking through Krystal's door, set my stuff down outside on the walkway against the wall and wondered how I could have forgotten. It was Bible study night. She'd begged me to come many times, especially the morning she picked me up from the hospital.

This Bible group wasn't the usual do-gooders, and that's what bothered me the most. It was a collection of tattooed freaks and pierced punks. Goth Christians. One of them stepped outside to smoke while I was still looking over the railing down at the parking lot. Fog covered everything and the lights at the entrance had rings around them in the haze.

They fed me dinner that night, vegan casserole. One guy kept farting and making people laugh. Everybody asked me personal questions, which I answered honestly, which surprised me, then pissed me off, and when I excused myself from the table to go crash on the couch, a chubby girl asked if she could pray for me.

"If you got to," I said.

The next day I went back to my parents' place.

"Who's breaking in?" Dad called from his bedroom.

"Just me."

"Go ahead and take it all."

There was a TV in my room that picked up a couple stations, and the days just dragged by. I knew I was going to need money for a lawyer. My first hearing, to set the date for the trial, was in a few days, and I figured it might be good to have somebody even for that. Walk in already lawyered up and shit.

Jones was a veteran of drunk driving charges. One time when he got pulled over, he stepped out of his van, forgetting there was a fifth in his lap, and sent the whiskey splashing all over the cop's feet. He got out of that one because the lawyer proved he'd done nothing to get pulled over in the first place. The attorney's name was Wesley, who everybody called Greasy Wesley because of the unbelievable help he'd given them. He was just the slime I needed.

I took the phone out of my dad's room and called Jones. He gave me the number before I even asked.

"Who you calling now?" my dad said through my door.

"Quit listening," I said.

"You'll need to quit talking for that to happen."

I turned the TV up and dialed. Wesley's secretary answered and talked me through a few questions about what I was facing.

"Can you turn down your TV?" she said. "It's difficult to hear you."

"No," I said, "I actually can't."

She finally transferred me to Wesley, and throughout the conversation he kept going on about, "Are you Darrel? You sure this isn't Darrel? Because you sound just like him." I said I wasn't Darrel, didn't know who Darrel was, and that this was the first time anything like this had happened to me. He said he'd see me in a couple days. "And one more thing," he said. "Bring half the money with you. I'll need the first half. And I'm real glad you're not Darrel."

I didn't have a quarter of the first half, but I said okay. Then I called the shelter again to see if they had any available shifts. The director, a pear-shaped man who wore loafers, asked how I was doing and said they'd been missing me. I felt the same around him as I did at my sister's place. He said he'd check the schedule and call me back. I called Jones again and begged for more gigs.

"It's no problem," he said. "We got a residency kind of thing going at Misty's. You're welcome anytime. We just figured that, you know, with your arm and all."

"I'll be there," I said. "My arm loves it."

The shelter didn't call back. We ended up playing a Thursty Thursdays gig the night before my first court date. It began at happy hour, some regulars just off work buying one-dollar bottles of Busch from the spray-painted refrigerator. After only a few songs, country standards with the same slow, swinging beat, pain splintered through my arm and down into the base of my spine.

I ordered a beer through the stage-right mic and when it came I chased down some painkillers with it. The mixture worked a little bit but mostly just fucked me up. The pain was still there, only now it seemed to be something on the outside of my body, a growth you could see. I got this idea it had a personality, that it and me were two different things.

Strumming over the muted strings of his acoustic, Jones counted us into one of his own songs about a girl and a dog. The feel was loose, but he made it interesting with a crosspicking pattern. The way it was written sounded like a letter. He was singing straight to some woman who'd left him: "It's hard work, keeping up an old house, with the memory of your hands and the taste of your mouth." It went on moping like that for a couple more verses—"I mowed the yard and made it look like new. Ain't it strange to see all this beauty without you"—then he got silly with it and I could see some smiles breaking out in the crowd. "Thank God I got a dog," he sang, "to cheer me up when I'm down. It makes me laugh when he gets a bath and goes running around." He kept on like that, really hamming it up, and I'd never seen such happiness in Misty's. He ended it by turning the lyrics unexpectedly back toward the song's beginning: "My dog is my savior. He's pretty stinky too. If it wasn't for him, every song I sing would be about you."

The crowd was clapping and I was slapping the body of my bass. "Jones Young, y'all!" I said into my mic, and a few people in the back whistled.

"Cheers, y'all," Jones said. "I been married once and divorced twice. Here's some Waylon."

And just when I was back into the bass, cruising and thumping along through the songs, just when I thought my buzz was here and could never end, in floated Jennifer. She hovered there bobbing her head along to the beat—my bass beat, the beat I was beating—and it didn't look like she'd seen me yet. My pain pulsed. Her hair was longer now and that was strange. It swung with her turning, bending, leaning. She was moving around like she was after something.

We were on our last song when Rachel showed up.

"Here's a situation," I said.

"What's wrong?" Jerry said. His shoulders were raised to a ride cymbal swing. "You look sick."

"My arm."

"All right," he said, "let's end this, boys."

Rachel came straight for the stage, doing some loopy dance with knees bent and her ass moving behind her like she was trying to fit into jeans tighter than the ones she was already wearing. Jennifer was watching her, then the Daffy Duck dude stepped over and talked into her ear. We tagged the end of the song and Jerry drove it right into the ground with a cymbal crash. He was a punk drummer and thought that gave him the right.

"Done," he said. "Let's go get drunk."

Rachel had danced right up to the stage, Jennifer still watching her. I shaped up my face, giving a handsome tight-jawed listen to what she was saying. She asked if she could get me a drink. On her. I said no and kept my periphery open. "They give the bands free Natties," I said.

"I *said,* can I get you a drink?"

I could see Jennifer over at the bar playing with Daffy, her hands everywhere. She talked in a loud, flat tone, and I knew she was faking it. She was calling for me.

Eventually Rachel said, "Just come to the bar with me and order for yourself."

I stepped off the stage, tripped and fell into a table. Bottles smashed and crashed and spun on the floor around me. I landed so hard on my bad arm that fire shot against the tip of my tailbone, the kind of pain that makes you laugh at first. Before I could understand what I'd done to myself, Jennifer was standing over me. "What the hell you think you're doing with my man?"

"Jennifer," I said. "Rachel."

"You know her name?" Jennifer said.

"And I know his," Rachel said.

I got to my knees. "Wait now."

"Sounds like you know more than that," Jennifer said.

"So does he," Rachel said.

"Calm down, y'all." I was holding on to a chair, trying to get up. "My arm hurts."

People were loud in the room and we couldn't really hear one another. I was standing there hurting like a motherfucker.

"How's about *I* go find out somebody's name?" Jennifer spun around and clattered back to the bar. The stool next to Daffy was open and she took it and went right into some conversation that was supposed to make me jealous. Talking and laughing and drinking. They hadn't earned any of it.

"And what was all that about?" Rachel said.

"Give me a cigarette."

"Excuse me?"

A trio of old-timers watched her leave. I knew not to follow her. Don't even look. These were guys who'd been sitting at the table I'd knocked into and were now mopping up the mess with napkins and wringing the hooch back into a glass. "He done it now," one said, looking from me to the closing door. "That's how they go," another said. "Wait now," the third one said, pointing at me. "You the feller knocked over them beers? I expect another one."

"Me too," I said, and ran to the door.

It was drizzling in the parking lot. Folks were huddled at a table, smoking under the big Bud Light umbrella. None of them was Rachel. I needed her for the battle Jennifer was mapping out inside, but her car was gone. I saw the dry gray patch where it had been, dark and wet all around it.

During the second set my arm sunk into some deep hurt. I

couldn't stay focused and it felt like my teeth were falling out. Jones's songs were good enough to keep me together for a while, but eventually shit started failing quicker than I could help. My fingers tingled when I plucked the strings, and I watched those two, Jennifer and Daffy, with a distant kind of hate. On the dance floor they stumbled into a broken two-step that nobody would've been jealous of except for me. I was playing on autopilot, buoyed and bobbing over the changes and trying my best to ignore what I seemed to be helping make happen. As the song ended, he tipped her from their two-step into a dip and I saw his biceps.

Silver was in his whiskers and his grin showed a dirty glint of gold. I decided it was time to report him.

By the end of the night, though, I didn't know where he'd gone to. Jennifer either. But I had an idea. I went out to Jones's van, found his cell phone on the floor and dialed.

"Nine-one-one. What is your emergency?"

It was a good question. I didn't know where to begin.

Eventually it became clear I didn't have an emergency. Just a bad-business claim. I even told them about the drugs, but they said, "Right. Look, if the guy's not there, what do you want us to do about it? We gotta catch him smoking it, selling it. What's his name?"

"I don't know. But you'll find everything if you just get over here."

"What does he look like? What was he wearing? Or driving? How will we know him?"

"He has tattoos. The one on his neck's Daffy Duck."

"Is this man's name Arnett?"

"I told you, I don't know his name."

"An officer is coming."

Jones packed up fast, saying he didn't want cops asking how

he planned on getting home, and since he was my only ride we rolled out before the law showed up.

It was a late winter day, clouds moving low and fast like they were being rewound. Mom let me use her car and I found a two-hour spot on the old square, right in front of the brick court-house where I was to be tried. Statues of Confederate heroes stood behind a short pyramid of cannonballs. I guess it was appropriate to have them out here, an encouragement to people like me: It's okay, we all lose eventually.

The district clerk's office was closed when I went up, so I walked down the block past the library and into the coffee shop a few streets over. I'd never been in the place before and had no idea anything this welcoming existed in Bordon. Thinking I might have to break out into some spontaneous genius shit in the middle of an argument in order to save my ass, I ordered four espresso shots. "Quadruple whammy," the teenage boy behind the register said. "No screwing around." He nodded like we shared something private. "Welcome to the quad squad."

I drank it walking back to my judgment day, and it got my heart racing and my stomach aching. A line a few folks long waited inside a hall. Before joining them, I rushed to the bath-room and let go of what the coffee had loosened. Considering the court fees I knew I'd be paying, I decided not to flush. As I left the stall, a man came in. He paused a moment, like someone had just insulted him, and said, "Ugh."

He walked back out and I followed behind him. His suit was wrinkled in the back from sitting. Turned out he was Wes-ley, my lawyer. He showed me to a cheap pew, then went up and stood near the judge's throne, opening his hands while he talked and closing them when he stopped. I'd hired him with the last of my little savings. In the corner, a projector screen showed a man in orange pleading not guilty to something he seemed very guilty of.

"That's not what I'm asking," the judge said to him. "I want to know if you'll be representing yourself or not."

"Ain't guilty!" The man stood up and did a doggie-paddle dance in his handcuffs. Some guards took him away and the screen went blue, like the room had suddenly filled with cartoon water. The whole episode made me feel better about my situation.

When my turn came, they set another date and Wesley got the out-of-state restriction dropped. "I'm free to go?" I said.

"For now."

"I can still drive and shit?"

"Innocent till proven," he said, bringing out a handkerchief and pulling at his nose with it.

"Probably lose my license, right?"

"We're still waiting on the blood tests."

I felt like an idiot for not knowing this was all that was going to happen. The spot on the street was still mine for another hour, but I didn't know what to do with myself and drove back home and slept the rest of the day.

The shelter finally called and I went in. A sex felon with eyes that moved quickly and independently of each other told me I'd made *Crime Times*. He kept up with the paper, looking for friends and family members he hadn't heard from in a while. "What the hell you been doing, huh?" he said. "You supposed to be an example for us shitheads, ya shithead."

"I know it," I said. "But listen, the charge is bogus. I didn't do anything. They pulled me over for false reasons."

He shook his head. "That mugshot of you," he said. "You look rough, bubby." Most of his teeth had been knocked out in prison, and here he was calling me rough. "If they do end up booking you," he said, "I'll write my cousin, make sure he don't give you no hard time."

"I appreciate that."

"And you ain't gotta worry—I won't tell nobody else."

"You're not the only one who reads that trash," I said.

"Maybe not, but I'm the only one that understands it."

After my shift I went looking for the paper. It wasn't a proud moment, walking into Joy Imperial and seeing my face on the front cover in the rack. I dropped it on the counter next to the six-pack I'd pulled from the cooler.

Rachel was working, and I hadn't looked up at her yet. "That all?" she said. She rang up the beer, put it in a plastic bag and then threw the paper in. "For free," she said.

"Didn't have to do that."

"I kinda do," she said. "It's like required. If you make it in, you get a free copy. Want another?"

"No thanks."

"It's not a bad picture," she said. "You look fine."

She, on the other hand, looked older since I'd last seen her. Maybe she was. She pushed the bag toward me and said, "Look on page three when you get home."

The beer was Dad's. He had a mini fridge in his room where he liked it kept. I took two and went to my room, cracked one open and scanned the paper till I found me, then turned to page three, and there was Daffy. From the front you could see only the fading bill on his neck. His name was Arnett Atkins.

Charged with video voyeurism. Felony.

Those nights at my parents' place, I lay fetal in bed and prayed to God for something good to happen in my life. Afterward I felt bad for even asking; I'd never requested a blessing for anyone else, but here I was, whimpering, *Please, more for me, I won't throw it away this time.* What worried me was that I didn't know if I'd actually be able to not throw it away. All matters lately seemed to slip through my fingers. Because of the prayers, I felt all the more deserving of what was happening to me. I didn't believe there would ever be an end to it, except maybe for the end.

One morning, Mom drove me to the Bordon library so I could check my email. She was going to run a few errands and come back in an hour to pick me up.

The library was clean and warm, like a classroom, and that made me feel out of place. I had a message from Jones in my inbox. He'd sent it almost a week ago, telling me to call him back as soon as I could. He'd been offered an opening slot to tour with Marshall Mac and the Deputies, a popular band around the state. Marshall liked to let his band spread out into long jams while he rapped about his tractor truck—some hillbilly hybrid rig. That was the title of his latest album: *Come Take a Ride in My Tractor Truck.* I asked the librarian if I could use the phone.

Jones answered on the first ring. "What's happening?" he said.

"Just got your email."

"Can you do it? I was worried about you."

"I'm all right." I almost jumped in the air. "You ain't found anybody yet?"

"This tour's going to be a long one. Most folks have lives."

"Suckers."

"Can you make practice every evening this week?"

"Yeah. Wait. I don't know. Where is it? I don't got a car yet."

"We're over in Ashland, still practicing in the storage unit. There's a couch to crash on. You can live here till we leave, for all I care. I've done it before."

I knew then that despite how selfish my prayers had seemed, they'd worked. "I don't want to take your bed."

"I've got the van. And the nests of a couple other birdies. Don't worry about me. I'll pick you up tonight. Bring a sleeping bag and a box of diapers."

I handed the phone back to the lady behind the desk. "I prayed for it," I told her. She was around my age but had the sorrowful smile of a woman who'd worked one job her whole life. "I prayed for it and I got it," I said. "I'm going to be opening for Marshall Mac."

"Never heard of him."

"That's okay," I said, and took her hand. "I can get you on the guest list."

She pulled away and studied me. "You're planning to play music with your arm like that?"

"Like what?" I said, and played some air bass at her.

Jones drove me over the mountain into Ashland. The van reeked of body odor, cigarettes and spilled beer, like it always had, but now I was part of the band and felt connected to the stink. The passenger bucket seat was sprung and I could feel the wires under me. We didn't listen to music or talk much, just kept the windows cracked with cigarettes burning.

The storage unit was packed to the air vents with instruments and sound gear. The couch against the sidewall was covered in set lists, notebooks, empty cigarette packs. I picked up a page full of words, and at the bottom there were some verses that hadn't been scratched out:

If I had my way I'd leave here tomorrow
Hitch up a ride and ride on down to Mexico
But there's just one thing I gotta do

"Don't read that," he said. "I don't go peeping through your stuff, do I?"

I dropped it onto a pile of duct tape and broken drumsticks.

"It ain't done yet," he said.

"What's it about? What's the one thing you gotta do?"

"That's what I'm figuring out. Anyway, it ain't about me."

He showed me around the room, where the light switch was and how to open the door with a crowbar from the inside. There was also a space heater that started throwing sparks if you left it on for more than three hours. "And if the cold doesn't wake you up," Jones said, "the smoke will."

After he left, I gathered his papers off the couch and made my bed. I read through his lyrics late into the night. Some of the songs I'd heard him sing before, and I could hear the melody behind the words. Others were new to me, a lot of pieces, verses and hooks. I'd never had the chance to look at anything like this. His songs seemed so simple that I never thought of the time he put into them. I decided I was going to play bass better than I ever had, just for him. This guy was good. He could be my escape.

The next morning I packed my sleeping bag into Jerry's bass drum and headed over to Hardee's for some coffee and a biscuit. I used as much free cream and butter and jelly as I could. When an employee came over and told me I had to quit taking the stuff, I tossed a packet of half and half into my mouth, chewed it up, swallowed the cream and spit the plastic into the countertop's trash hole.

"You're the only dude in the world who this bothers," I said. "How does that feel?"

We practiced from the afternoon until midnight, drinking beer and eating pizza, then we were loading equipment into the back of the Econoline, the last bench taken out for amps and instruments and drums and sleeping stuff. I was carrying a bag of pedals with the hand of my broken arm when a flash of pain lit me up and dropped me to my knees. Jones came running but I said I was fine, just tripped, didn't need any help getting up.

Our first show was in Lloyd at a country store that let us sleep upstairs in the attic afterward. Only if you don't drink, said the woman who booked the gig. Yes ma'am, we said, and hauled out a fifth the second we heard her close the downstairs door. It had been a long drive for a low-paying gig—just enough for gas, really—while Mac and the Deps got hotel rooms and backstage sandwiches they didn't even look at. We lay hungry and happy in that attic. One window at the end of the low-angled room showed the ink-colored night sky. We carried on with the kind of talk appreciated only by those creating it at the moment— women, somebody taking too long with the bottle, somebody else claiming to have lost it until we found it stashed in the foot of his sleeping bag and smacked him around a little, all of us laughing like boys beneath the raw-pine beams.

"What we need now is girls," somebody mumbled as sleep settled down over us, the last words of the night, the single thought on all our minds, wondering what tomorrow's gig might bring.

The drive wasn't far, just a couple hours southwest over the Tennessee border. We got there to find Mac's group already backlined. Two roadies were standing on the unlit stage noodling around on guitars. The venue was an old theater with a bar in back, four young ladies wiping tap nozzles with washcloths, wrapping silverware in napkins and dancing around. Sound-check was for them, and it was the best we'd played so far.

The soundman had a key ring the size of a jailer's, and because of this we knew we could trust him. "Go get y'all something to chew on and swallow," he said once the levels were set. "First two drinks are free. And the blonde, if you drop shit on her side of the bar, any damn thing at all, money or glasses or whatever, she'll bend over and pick it up for you. Make sure you drop something."

We bellied up and ordered burgers. When the blond girl handed out our drinks, Jones pushed a couple quarters over the edge of the bar and said, "Oops." Then Jerry's whole wallet hit the floor. She put her fists on her hips and said, "You been talking with Henry."

Everybody laughed except me. She noticed that and winked before going back into the kitchen, leaving the money and the wallet on the floor.

"That was at you, Leon," Matt said. "You dog."

"It's only because of his arm," Jerry said.

The monitors gave a sharp clarity to the sound, and somewhere in the middle of the set I listened to what we were doing and thought, Not too bad for a bunch of losers.

After the set, I met the blond girl out on the side of the building. She kicked the wall randomly while we talked. Everybody else left for the Motel 6 but I stuck around with her, drinking top-shelf liquor. Vodka and gin infused with herbs. I'd never had anything like it. We went back to her house, and the sex was just two sloppy bodies being tossed against each other: a late-night mistake that sobered me up enough so that I couldn't sleep. The thickness of the girl's thigh as I slapped it, the smack echoing in my head, the sound of her dropping her boots on the wood floor next to the bed, the sheets smelling of perfume, beer, barroom chemicals and other dudes.

She was unconscious when I decided to go. The room was so quiet it hurt, a loud rushing static in my ears that wouldn't quit. I slipped into my boots and out the door. The ground felt too hard as I walked past strip malls through a cold drizzle. My head throbbed. I never wanted to see her again. I wouldn't.

I didn't have a cell phone, and it was early enough I expected everybody to be asleep when I got back. I figured I'd have to pound on the door and wake them all up. But that wasn't the case. Jones was crouched against the wall outside the room smoking a cigarette and blowing out big clouds in front of him. "Where the F." He shook his head. "Have you been? I don't care what you been doing with what's-her-ass. Well, actually I do."

"Come on," I said. "It was like being in a washing machine."

Normally he would've laughed. "People been calling for you. A lady named Barbara? Rachel's mom? Says she's gone."

"Who? Her or Rachel?"

Jones scraped his Camel across the sandy cement and left it smoking at his feet. "Rachel," he said. "The one that wasn't calling me on the phone."

I was so hungover that I could hardly make sense of what he was saying. The sun shellacked everything and made Jones look like an old picture. It felt like a memory—me standing there looking at him, and him telling me, "She's gone, man. The girl you were sleeping with? She's missing."

"Slept with," I said. "One time."

"Well, apparently there's a whole search party. Cops, the news, everybody. And it's not looking good."

"I didn't kill her."

"Didn't say you did."

"I know what you're thinking."

"That's not what I'm thinking. Nobody thinks you did it. If they did, believe me, you'd know. It's just—it sounds like some folks are saying you were the last one with her."

"Who's saying that?"

"Barbara."

"Who told her?"

Jones looked at me, put his hands on his knees and pushed himself up. "I got no fucking idea."

The next few nights were the same thing in different places. I kept expecting to see a detective peeking around a corner, but it was just more shows, long van rides, the occasional after-party with drunken scene queens taking bids from dudes in bands. I got one in West Virginia and ended it by leaving her in a basement apartment on a bare mattress next to a leaking water heater. Everyone else was sleeping upstairs. I hid in the van.

I didn't know who had the keys but that was okay. I still loved Jennifer. I felt bad about hooking up with Rachel, and that's what made me drink and sleep around. I felt guilty for whatever happened to her and couldn't stand the idea of being questioned. I didn't want to think or talk about any of it. As long as it stayed buried, it wouldn't walk.

I was packed into a sleeping bag wearing all my clothes, on the floor between the two bench seats. The horn honked—someone locking and unlocking the doors from outside. When I opened an eye, the water bottle in front of my face was frozen solid. Something bad was happening inside my cast. The side door slid open and Jones said, "Ain't you freezing to death?" He had layers of sweaters beneath his denim jacket, and the bright winter sun cast a shadow from his cap's bill over his face. He said the girl had woken them up last night looking for me. Jerry went to bed with her just to shut her up. "Took one for the team," Jones said. "I guess you've been out here?"

"I can't move," I said. "I'm paralyzed."

"That good, huh? Damn. Might go get me some."

"It's all in my spine and shit," I said.

He put his hand on my foot and told me to move it. I did. "You're all right," he said. He helped me sit up, then touched above my cast and asked if I could feel it. That whole side of my body burned and his touch left the spot pulsing and smoldering. Sticking out the other end of the cast, my fingers looked like cooked sausages ready to split.

"Well," he said, lighting a cigarette and blowing smoke into the van. "It's not paralysis. But it ain't good, either."

He drove me to the closest emergency room, where the doctor said the break hadn't healed properly, that it was actually still broken and breaking even more. A line of fracture had traveled up the bone, zigzagging like a slow bolt of lightning. That's how he described it. "What have you been doing?" he said. "You've been letting it rest, yes?" His name was Dr. Franklin.

"I been playing bass," I said.

"For a country band," Jones said. "That shouldn't kill him."

"Country music won't kill you," the doctor said. "But I've known it to ruin folks' lives."

Neither of us could tell if he was joking.

His diagnosis, though, was simple: I couldn't finish the tour. He said he was glad I was in so much pain. "Seems to be the only thing you're liable to listen to," he said.

"But I got nothing back home," I told him. "I prayed for this tour. It happened." I didn't know why I was confessing my life to him, except that he was a man who didn't know me and it felt good pleading for another chance to a person with some power. "This wasn't the plan," I said.

He wrote me a generous prescription for painkillers, and a drive-through drugstore filled them quick as an order of fries. I sold half the pills to Jerry and bought a Greyhound ticket back to Bordon. The tour had almost a month left and I knew I couldn't hold up. I told them to hang on to my bass, in case they found somebody else, but it was really because it hurt so bad to even put the strap over my shoulder.

"We'll hold on to it for ya," Jones said.

Jerry flipped his cell phone closed. "We got a bassman coming right now," he said.

And there I was, standing at the station with a duffel bag of clothes by my feet. Nobody looked back from the van. They just drove away leaking a cloud of exhaust.

My sister was at the Shell station eating an ice-cream cone when my bus arrived. "Oh, my goodness," she said. "What all did you see? What was it like out there?"

"Sucked," I said.

"What's it like to be back?"

"Sucks more," I said.

When she took the 231 split, I asked where she was going. "I don't need any errands. Just rest."

"Well," she said. "Let's see," she said. "Mom and Dad are—"

"Don't do this to me."

"They're doing a lot better lately."

"I can't. I'll go crazy."

"Sure you can," she said, holding back tears, her mouth all tight and warped. "I'm the one who can't. I'm doing this for *you.*" Then she started crying so hard that she had to pull over onto the shoulder, cars swooshing by. When I asked what was wrong she hit the steering wheel with both hands, screamed and sent a sharp pain through me that I imagined looked like the bolt Dr. Franklin had described. "Can't you take this serious for one minute?" she said. "You are losing your life. You're throwing it away. You could change, you know. Use this as a chance to become better. Ahh! I don't know."

I knew what she meant. I'd tried my hardest the whole twelve-hour bus ride to figure out how this could make me strong. But the pain pills were stronger, and every time I thought of improving myself I ended up seeing Rachel. I wanted to tell Krystal about her, but I was worried about sounding guilty for something I didn't do. Plus everything I had done.

I didn't go to my final court date. I stayed in my shitty bed in my shitty old bedroom. The band would have been back by now, and I felt time funneling by so fast that I feared I was caught in some sucking drain. One day Mom came into my room carrying a warrant for my arrest.

"This came in the mail," she said.

"I didn't do it."

"You missed court," she said. "I understand. Your arm's broken. You're scared." Then she took me to the clinic where she worked, had a doctor look at my arm and write up a report about our emergency visit and date it for my missed court appearance.

He handed her the letter and she thanked and thanked him until he said, "You earned it."

She looked at me to see if I'd caught that. "What?" she said. "It's a hard job."

"I'm sure it is," I said to the doctor.

A changed date. Other than more court fines, the note had worked. My mom expected me to be grateful for the favor, but I couldn't ignore the favors she'd already given to him.

The trees outside started turning green. It depressed me, the seasons changing while I stayed the same. Mom kept quiet and then came into my room one day asking why I wasn't working yet.

"Because I don't have a fucking job," I told her.

She reached behind the dresser and pulled the plug on the TV. "Go cut the grass."

I went out to the garage and gassed and primed the mower. Starting it with one hand was a son of a bitch, but I got it going and was pushing it crookedly through the yard when I ran over a nest of bunny rabbits. The cut length was set high and I don't think I hurt any of them. They were right there at my feet now, squirming in their little roofless burrow, eyes barely open. Imagine if the first thing you saw in this world was those enormous blades spinning above you and my dumb ass just standing there. I left the mower and went back inside.

"You already done?" Mom said. Her hair was big from brushing.

"There's life and shit all over the place out there," I said.

"You ain't thought about nobody but yourself since day one."

"I'm twenty-five fucking years old," I said. "I've thought about a lot of people. Lots of different people. Animals even. Squirrels. Rabbits."

Then she just dumped it on me. "And what about this missing girl? Where'd you put her?"

I left the room and let her stew with those words. She knew I was innocent. "Your son's going to kill himself!" I yelled, then slammed the door and started walking.

I was back living in the same rat-matted shithole, my one real girlfriend had blown me off, and as long as Rachel didn't show up, nobody wanted to be seen with me. I was guilty around town. I could just feel the suspicion.

I considered applying to the army and catching some air in a humvee over a sand dune while a dirty city burned behind me. But there was the arm thing.

That cast eventually came off but the bone was still fucked.

The nurse that sawed the plaster apart told me to relax and wait to see how it healed. If I tried to push things, the bass might be off my shoulders forever.

That spring I did a lot of walking without ever knowing where I was going. I'd follow the train tracks for miles, stopping to inspect various dead critters. Once I found a turkey vulture trapped inside a deer's ribcage, the bones picked clean and the spine arching over the bird with the ribs bending down around it. I couldn't understand how it ever got itself into such a mess, but there it was, totally stuck. I tried to push the skeleton over, but a piece of bone had wedged between the rail and a tie. The vulture growled out a stream of puke and let off a gassy stink. I kicked and pulled until the skeleton broke free, and the vulture hobbled out, its wing broken and hanging loose at its side. "Go!" I said. "You're free. Get!" But it just kind of stayed there, staring at me through the side of its head.

Other times I'd sit on the guardrail of the highway and watch the vehicles blow by. I'd hope for somebody to stop, but nobody ever did.

One day I decided I wasn't coming home until I found a job. There weren't that many places to look, and I needed something close enough to walk to. I didn't get far before my shirt was plastered to my back. No breeze in this bowl of a town. The sky was the color of steam and I was careful not to stay out in it too long. The road I was walking down narrowed and cars went swerving and honking past me. I dropped into Foodville for the AC and hung out in the front near the smokes until this man asked if I needed help finding something.

"Yeah," I said. "A job."

"Aisle six," he said.

I looked in that direction, and he said, "Just kidding. Follow me."

We went into his office. He talked while I looked out the two-way mirror; none of the customers knew I was watching. The next day he put me on bagging.

I worked part-time, not enough to save anything, but Dad got pissed when he heard I'd found work and asked if I thought I was better than he was. I did, but I didn't tell him that. He bought dime bags from our neighbor that stunk like ammonia and spent his working hours with a cloud of blue smoke above his head. I almost asked him if he'd heard about Rachel until one day he did it for me.

"I heard Carol talking?" he said. "About that girl you lost?"

"Which one?"

He nodded off, and then shook his head, either to wake himself up or simply to disagree with the sudden, unwelcome consciousness. Choked by the smell of the chair he slumped in, I asked him to tell me more. He clicked his tongue as if trying to decide whether to play a hand or fold.

"Forget it," I said.

"I almost did."

Summertime, and our yard was going wild. The mower was where I'd left it, stuck in its own track, and I figured the rabbits had built a little bunny kingdom under there by now. I kept my job at Foodville because the AC was reliable.

I started a beard, didn't trim it, kept it rough, and looked at myself in windows whenever I got the chance. My left arm still hurt when I tried to straighten or flex it, the muscle withering and the whole thing shriveling. It looked like somebody had accidentally put the wrong part on my body, and I made sure to turn so I could only see my right side. I pretended I didn't know who I was and rated myself on a scale of one-to-ten handsomeness. When I was honest I never made it past five. But if I glanced in the perfect direction, my teeth spreading below that darkening mustache, my right arm strong and straight, I could almost see myself as somebody worthy of Jennifer.

One morning after I'd just unlocked the grocery's doors, I was looking in the window and thinking I might be moving into a six when this girl comes up to the other side of the window. I was looking at myself, and she steps right into my reflection. I didn't recognize her at first. She was wearing a hoodie, long jeans, work boots. It was ninety damn degrees outside. The store hadn't been open ten minutes. She walked in and squinted around.

It was Jennifer, heading for the dairy wall.

A man old enough to be her dad came in behind her and stood in the doorway. He wasn't even wearing a shirt. His chest was dark and at first it looked like he had some kind of wing tattoo below his collarbone, but then I saw it was a rug of hair. He asked if he could come in, and before I said no, he did. I realized it was a chest full of tattoos, of chest hair, or small feathers, or flames. A hand-done job, that was all I could really tell. The hair hanging from his head was real, and on his neck was Daffy Duck. Arnett Atkins had arrived.

Not a whole lot had changed for me since last winter, and those moments at Misty's felt far gone and up close all at once. Rachel hadn't yet floated to any surface. She occupied a small place in my mind, like some bad dream that wasn't possible to confront. But Arnett—had he heard I was the one who'd turned him in?

Jennifer was reaching for something high on the wall.

"The fuck you looking at?" Arnett said. He leaned in, and I could smell beer on his breath, a gamey odor from his flesh.

"That girl," I said. "Nothing."

"Who are you?" he said. "And why?"

I didn't answer.

"That's what I thought. I classify this situation NFI: Not Fucking Important. Mommy's little hunchy boy."

I straightened up. "What'd you just say?"

"Put down your feathers, banty." Arnett's eyes wouldn't keep still. They were wet and he pulled a rag from his pants and wiped them. He was taking in everything except me, his jugular pulsing through the skin of his neck. He held a hand in front of his face, stared into his palm, brought it to his mouth, licked it. He smiled and revealed a dark space in the side of his mouth. Teeth were missing since I'd last seen him. His bottom ones were thin and burnt-looking like used matches. All the gold in the back molars, gone. His tongue filled a gap and his eyes rolled back like something was moving inside him. "Let's start over again, okay?" he said. "I'll give you another chance, yes? Here's a better question. What do you want to be?"

"That's deep," I said.

"Answer the fucking question, hunch."

Maybe he actually didn't recognize me. "I don't know," I said.

"That's your problem. You need to make a decision."

"About what?"

Arnett sucked a finger and cleaned his ear with it. "Your store. Keep an eye on it. Good old workingman boy. You do your job and she'll do mine."

He went to the bright wall where she stood. She seemed tiny in those baggy clothes, probably his. They talked and he threw his thumb behind his head. She glanced in my direction, then covered her face and turned away. He took her by the shoulder and said something into the hair dangling from her hood and all down her face. She shook her head. Finally he let her go and she walked straight for me over the shining floors I'd mopped that morning before opening.

"Look at you," I said.

"Look at me." She kept her head down until she reached my checkout counter. "What the hell'd you just say to him?" She put her hands down on the conveyor belt and it started moving, pulling her closer.

"Find everything you need, ma'am?" I said.

She laughed. She was beautiful. Then she spun away again and the color left her face. Her eyes screwed shut with exhaustion, and lines cracked through her skin. "Listen," she said, and I turned off the belt. "He told me to tell you to quit thinking what you're thinking."

"He doesn't know what I'm thinking."

"But he knows what you want."

"Who is he to you?"

"He's my . . . Well."

Arnett was wandering up the aisle with a quart of milk. I wrote my parents' phone number on the back of a receipt, the numbers crossing over the print of a half-off coupon for hickory-smoked ham hocks. She stuffed the paper into her pocket and said, "What happened to your arm?"

"Call me and I'll tell you."

She pushed through the door to leave, before the motion sensor had time to swing it open.

There were still sweaty fingerprints on the black rubber belt. Her hands were always damp. It was something I'd forgotten about.

"What's the holdup?" Arnett said, setting the milk where her hands had been.

I turned on the switch. "You want a bag for this, sir?"

"Yeah," he said. "I'd love a fucking bag."

I waited days, but she didn't call and I figured I'd freaked her out. Then she did, and she sounded scared, but I told her to hold on for a minute and went into my dad's room. Standing over him, I said, "Your disability came through." He didn't budge. So far as I could tell, he was free of all worries. Percocet, beer, a couple joints—that's the kind of place that helps you forget you have a wife who'll wipe your mouth clean but won't kiss you goodnight. I stepped over piles of dirty clothes and unplugged the phone he kept on the carpet between his bed and the wall.

I talked to her in my room with the door locked and a pillow over my face to insulate the sound. In bursts of muffled weeping, she told me Arnett was at it again only this time it was even worse. She talked until the phone got hot against my ear. "Jennifer," I said, "slow down. What exactly's going on?"

"A whole damn lot," she said. "It's all—I don't know—everything."

While she was busy not telling me, I heard Mom's tires in the gravel driveway. Car door shutting. Storm door slamming. "Come over," I said. "Tomorrow."

She asked where I was living and I told her. "Oh," she said, "that place."

I told her we'd have my room to ourselves, with one parent at work and the other in bed. I could hear Mom in the hallway now, dropping her purse and kicking off her shoes. I told Jennifer I'd even pay for the gas, fill up her tank.

"I'll be there early," she said.

Our connection crackled when the line in my parents' room got plugged in. "I'll see you then," I said.

She'd hung up by the time Mom was on the line saying, "Hello? Hello? Is somebody there? I can hear you breathing."

She sounded so hopeful, like it might've been someone calling from her past, when she was young and innocent, or from her future, when she would be rescued from this house and these two useless men. I didn't have the heart to let her down, so I just listened. "I know you're there," she said. "Who are you?"

I couldn't sleep that night, and the next morning I'd barely closed my eyes when I heard Mom calling for me outside. Early sunlight on the floor. Dizzy from getting up so fast, I jumped out the back door and limped and hopped around the house over the gravel. Mom was standing in front of her car and staring at this mutt of a pickup rumbling and crunching into the driveway, a white Chevy cab with a black Ford bed angled behind it. The whole thing rattled in disagreement with itself. Jennifer sat behind the wheel, her hair up in rubber bands just how I liked it.

"Don't even tell me," Mom said. "I don't need to know." She got in her car and pulled out around the truck, leaving tracks in the wet morning grass.

Jennifer kicked the door shut and checked in her purse for something. She always did this when she was buying time to think about what to say. Seeing her standing there was like watching the last half-year dissolve. Maybe everything was cool. Here she was, here I was. Nothing different, nothing new. She took a bottle from her purse. It was purple glass without a label, not much bigger than her hand. She shook it at me and said, "This could be the answer."

I led her inside my dark place. Dad kept the blinds shut, and the window unit in the living room was surrounded with strips of cardboard duct-taped to the glass and covering up any space light might slither through. I usually didn't notice this, but once she stepped through the door it was like I was experiencing the house for the first time. The old kitty litter in the carpet, left over from our dead cat. The smell of Hamburger Helper in the walls.

"Sorry," I said. "I'm moving out soon."

"Why? You'll just end up right back here."

"Shh," I said. "We got to be quiet." I took her hand and led her down the hallway to my room, shut the door and pushed in the lock.

"We got to be quiet anywhere we go," she said.

"Where you living? Are you safe?"

It took her a while to get to it. "I'm staying with that guy, Arnett, in an abandoned inn. Right at the top of that stupid mountain."

"Which one?"

"The stupid one." She pointed past the wall.

"They're all stupid," I said. "Why're you out there?"

"Renovating. Nobody knows we're there," she said. "Nobody even goes up there. It's on Nitro." She was still wearing her sunglasses, but I could see her right eye was dark and swollen.

"He a lefty?" I said.

"Good thing you're not," she said, looking at my arm.

"I broke it the night you left me."

"And it still ain't healed?"

"It keeps breaking."

"Just like your little heart," she said.

"It's not funny. I wrecked my truck chasing after you and Greg."

"Greg," she said. "He seemed like a good idea at the time. Smart guy, you know?"

"I don't care anymore. Are you okay?"

"We been renovating," she said. "We can do whatever we want with the building. Nobody gives a shit."

"How long you been with this guy?"

"Since he lost his job at Misty's. That's about the time we met. He doesn't know how the cops figured out what he was doing. They found cameras. They were, like, in the bathrooms or something." She looked away when she said it.

"Why the hell'd you follow him up to Nitro?"

"The cameras weren't his. Swears he doesn't know how they got there."

"So just to prove he's not up to any illegal shit he breaks into somebody's place."

"It's his," she said. "Or used to be his dad's. Whoever owns it's letting him live up there. We even have animals. Dogs, pigs. You know, real animals. It's, like, ours. He's happy. I'm not going to spell it out for you."

"Maybe I'm missing something. What brought you here to me?"

"You're definitely missing something."

"Yeah," I said. "You."

She took off her glasses. A bag of dark skin cradled a blood-shot eyeball. "I never see anybody," she said. "Arnett does most of the work on the place. I just sweep things up and stay out of his path. We hooked a keg to one of the old taps, so the downstairs bar is kind of running now. We started it as a business."

"I thought nobody goes up there."

"It's in case they do."

"Does he know you're here?"

"You kidding? Hell no. He thinks I'm running errands. Which I am."

"Why're you with him?"

"Because. He had what I needed when I needed it. That and he makes me think of somebody I knew one time." She turned her head away from what she was thinking about and looked out the window. She pushed it up, and heat rolled in like she'd just opened an oven. She lit a cigarette, blew smoke at the screen and tapped her ash onto the sill.

"Does he have a crew?" I said.

"Sure needs one," she said, and then stopped to consider the idea. "He's working by himself right now. You ever work carpentry?"

"I'm no good," I said, lifting my hurt arm as far as it would go.

"He needs a few bums he can pay to swing hammers. If you know anybody."

"Me," I said.

"Would you do it?"

"Only joking."

"He probably wouldn't even remember you. He was still high from the night before, that morning we came into the store. Sorry about that. I didn't know you were working there."

"I'm glad it happened. You need help."

"You should shave your beard, just to make sure."

"Like it?"

"Doesn't matter. It's got to go."

"I'll think about it."

When she left, I lay facedown on the floor, sniffing where she'd been sitting. I didn't think she actually wanted me working up there, and until I was certain that she did I wasn't planning on shaving or doing much of anything.

I went to Foodville that afternoon but I was hardly there. About an hour before closing, my boss came out of his office. "It wasn't even busy," he told me, "but you *made* it busy. You had a line an aisle long. You look tired—go get some sleep."

Mom was already gone to work and I was eating stale cereal from the box when Jennifer knocked. I told her to wait and went to check on my dad. He was drinking beer and didn't look up when I came in.

"Jennifer's here," I said.

"Send her in."

"We're going to talk. Alone. You need anything before I close my door?"

"Jennifer'll do. We could all of us," he said, "just sleep like little puppies together."

In my room she lifted up her shirt. Scars covered her belly and up toward her breasts. Not surgical-looking, just puckered things that still needed healing. I leaned over and touched one. My finger looked young next to it.

"Kind of numb," she said.

"Can you feel this?" I traced the shape of hurt flesh. Some of the crests were still scabbed.

"Only if I'm watching." She pushed her shirt back down. "I meant to show you yesterday."

"What the hell?"

She told me that when she and Arnett first moved into the inn she tried to leave him, but he tied her to a board and brought her out to the pen where they kept the pigs and the dogs. All the animals lived together and it drove them crazy. He dropped her down into it and dumped slop all over her. The hogs came out of the barn and went straight for the feed. The dogs stayed back, whining and yapping. When she started bleeding, he shot a rifle into the air and sent the hogs running. Then he asked if she really planned on leaving him. "He shoots the air a lot," she said.

I'd heard some shit about what people did to each other, but this beat all of it.

She pushed down the waist of her jeans and showed me another one. I studied what Arnett had done to her and considered my options.

"What are you going to do about it?" I said.

"Don't know."

"Can't you call somebody? Make a report or something."

"What if he tries stopping me?"

"Tries is different than stopping." I got up.

"Where *you* going?" she said.

"Call the cops."

"Please, please don't," she said. "Oh, please. Don't. You can't." She dropped to her knees and grabbed my hands. "They won't hold him long enough. He'll come and find me. I mean, even after they found the cameras, he's still out. He'll probably end up going to jail once he's convicted. But Jesus, it takes so long. And for this there's no proof."

"Your body's proof."

She covered her ears. "I don't want to be anybody's proof," she said. "He'll get me back. He'll find me, and if he knows I'm even talking to anybody . . . Oh, God. I'm nobody's proof."

I turned the volume up on the TV so Dad couldn't hear us. I sat down next to her on the bed.

She handed me the same bottle she'd shown me when she'd first arrived yesterday. "This," she said.

"For what?"

And she said: "To kill him."

The bottle held a homemade embalming fluid, for when Arnett shot animals. "He makes the stuff," she said. "Swallow it just a little bit and you'll die." She looked at her nails. "Drink him with it."

We looked into each other's eyes. She sat directly in front of me in the messy nest of a sheet. Our legs were crossed, knees touching. I laid the bottle down beside us like it might explode. She filled my palms with her fists. The whole world was easily fixed. I felt more needed than I ever had in all my life.

"This is your idea," I said.

"I was just thinking out loud," she said. "But you look interested."

We stayed in my room all day, watching TV and talking and touching and watching more TV and touching. I heated Chinese in the microwave. While we were eating, I asked her how she was allowed to stay gone so long, and she said he sometimes let her get made up in town. "I'll hit the Hairport after this," she said. "Get my hair and nails and lips and toes done."

Some real shit was playing on *Unsolved Mysteries*. She turned off the TV and the noise of summertime droned and knocked against the window, the static of wings and legs and hard knobby bodies, millions of them, all zipping around and fighting for that same old thing.

We lay close together but I was afraid if I reached out to touch her I wouldn't be able to feel her at all. She sat up. "Grab me a beer?"

When I got back, her clothes were thrown next to the bed with the sheet across her bottom half. Another piece of hurt bloomed on her white belly. That place that had once been pure and untouched. I couldn't stand it. She reached for the cold long-neck, took a swallow and told me to sit down.

"You wanna see something?" She pulled her iPhone out of her jeans on the floor and spider-fingered through lit menus of options. The screen flipped to unfocused darkness. "Watch this."

The sound of random noise came through the little speaker. The image now had a bright spot in the middle. I couldn't tell what was happening but the noise eventually made sense. It was the barroom clatter of Durty Misty's. Right here in the stupid little bedroom of my life. The screen darkened again and the image came into focus. Short tapered pillars of sitting thighs. The drawn line and darkened thatch through the middle of a lady's ass. There was a sloppy kiss mark on one cheek, a tattoo labeled *Kiss My Ass.*

Rachel's.

"Sexy-looking stuff," Jennifer said. "Isn't it?" She held out the phone like the video was something a person of talent had made.

"How recently was this taken?" I said.

"I don't know. Arnett showed it to me last night. I went ahead and asked about the cameras—you know, after we talked about it?—and he just hauled it out and showed it to me. This phone's his. He doesn't know I took it. I'm going to throw it away."

Rachel started peeing.

Jennifer touched my knee and walked her hand like a beetle up my thigh. "So," she said, "maybe he was lying about the cameras." Her hand went from my leg to her crotch. "He's an asshole, but I do like watching this stuff. Doesn't it kinda turn you on?"

"No," I said. "This is serious."

"I just can't believe he was actually doing it behind my back. I mean, *you*'d never do anything like this."

"If I wanted to I would," I said. "But I don't. That's the difference. Do you know who that is there?"

Rachel finished, the last bit dripping from her hairs, no wiping, just a quick finger tap over her slice. "Some girl," Jennifer said. "That ain't the point."

"You've never seen her?"

"Who?"

"That girl," I said, touching the phone.

Rachel's butt left the bowl and the video paused on her pulling her jeans halfway up, and like that she was gone. Jennifer said, "I can't go around asking every woman I see, 'Will you please pull your pants down?' That might sound weird."

I thought about it. No cops this time. They'd had enough of me, and me of them. Jennifer was right. We could handle this on our own.

"What are you thinking about right now?" she said.

But I couldn't tell her I knew that ass. "That girl could've been you," I said. "That's what I'm worried about. It could be any of these girls," I said, pointing past the wall and out into the world.

"Why would he video me?" she said. "He's seen it all in person. Anyway, listen, the real problem's this." She showed me a wound on her hip that looked like a gigantic nightcrawler twisting out from under her skin.

"I'll do anything," I said. "We got to get you away from him."

"I already told you. He likes drinking those slurpees from the station. He mixes vodka into that shit. It's his cocktail. All we do is add a little something else." She flicked the bottle, her fingernail clicking against the glass. "We could be safe loving each other. We can't even love each other right, me and you."

She held her breasts in her hands and weighed them. Despite the scars from the pigs, the full round nipples were there, dark and unbitten. She lay back and told me to come heal her. It didn't feel real but I did it anyway. I had no choice anymore, now that I was on her, outside my body, and inside hers.

After, my head in her lap, her finger drawing on my ear, she said, "I seen shit like this in detective movies. The thing that gets you is the cops tracing the killing back to some kind of deal."

"You ever tell the cops about what he did to you?"

"Never told nobody shit."

"But people know y'all were together."

"Are," she said. "Are together. You got to do it. Get close to him. Get him in a situation where he sees you as the giving type. You call my phone and I'll let you talk to him."

"But he'll know something's up if I'm calling your number."

"I'll tell him tonight I met somebody looking for work. Ran into you outside the Hairport. When you talk to him, tell him that. And tell him about the trouble you been in. Lost your license. He'll like that part. Tell him you're needing work. Make everybody see you as being on his side."

The Lookout was a four-story disaster, twisting clapboard siding and slate shingles sliding off the roof, the whole thing leaning just below the peak of Nitro Mountain. Arnett had set up ladders and scaffolding all over the place. I was using my bad arm to steady myself, climb, hold nails straight, even pull away siding. I spent most of my working hours up around the roof, beneath the sun's nose. I could look down over my shoulder and see the scab that was Bordon, the infected area around it, and past that the curve of the earth.

Stilted behind me on the last rocky incline was that tower with the red light. I'd grown up gazing at it, wondering what it was, but even now, being so close to it, I still didn't have much of an idea. Planes never flew near here. Just some souvenir left by the coal company.

The mountain had a different name before Nitro. I'd heard old-timers call it Paran. But that was before coal miners hollowed it out and created air pockets that made the ground unfit to stand on, not to mention all the explosives they'd left behind in those tunnels. By now the county had condemned it.

I'd never been any closer than the highway or had any reason to risk stepping on that forsaken land, but I'd ended up doing exactly what Jennifer said. I called Arnett, explained myself and asked if he'd let me work for him.

"Jennifer told me about you," he said. "We know each other?"

"Nah."

"Good. Let's do a trial run. See if you're desperate enough."

My parents' house was a dozen miles down the road from the Lookout's front access, and Arnett picked me up in Jennifer's truck that same day. Bouncing and bottoming out along the dusty trail back up, he said, "There'll have to be a lot of training before I actually start paying you."

"That's all right. I'm a quick study."

"That's what she said."

That night he got too drunk to drive me home and decided to keep me on. Anyway, he needed another worker to make the project look real. According to him, the place had once been his uncle's and he now believed it ought to be his, but blood rights didn't mean much in the legal world. He wouldn't say more than that. We were hanging out in the downstairs bar and he asked if I'd ever been in a strip club, a whorehouse, anywhere. "The bar's where it all goes down."

His face was swollen to the point of looking like he'd been stung by some huge insect. He also owned guns. A lot of them. Since moving up here, he'd developed the habit of going killing—not hunting—and then preserving the corpses with homemade embalming fluids, filling the rooms upstairs with them. A few days in, prying away some rotten wood, I peeked into a window and saw busts of bucks, flying geese, a fox forever frozen in the motion of running. Some were mounted on the walls, most just piled on the floor, a few already rotting. The next window gave a view into Arnett and Jennifer's bedroom, where a hog and a dog hung together by wires in a screeching position above the bed.

It turned into a week of fluorescent green mountains, the sickly scent of pines, vistas so high my stomach turned. I was working up on the ladder one day when a vulture floated past and brushed my ear with its wing. "Hello, my friend," I said. It glided away, combing the clouds with its feathers. "I knew you'd make it."

When I looked down, Arnett was watching me. "I bet it's hard jerking off up there, ain't it?" he said. "Oh, I'm a very fine person." He went away for a while and came back carrying a long-barreled shotgun. I tried not to fall off the ladder. "Get down here and follow me," he said.

We walked behind the barn to the pigpen and I kept my distance. When I caught up, he told me to get on my knees. "Look under there," he said, pointing at where the wall met the ground. I could see a possum hiding in the washout. It had purple ears and pink fingertips. "Scare it out of there," he said.

I took a shovel and kind of rolled the thing into the light. It moved like its eyes hurt, probably trying to decide whether to play dead or make a run for it. Arnett pumped the action, pulled the trigger and the little guy's entire head just went poof into a wet cloud, the blast cracking and echoing down the valley.

I did what he told me, broke some dead branches over my knee, dropped them in a metal trash can lid, sprinkled some gasoline over it and got a fire going. Arnett gutted and skinned the possum. I stretched chicken wire across the lid over the coals. When it was cooked, Arnett divided up the smoking carcass onto two plastic plates and poured vinegar and beer all over his. He pulled a handful of wild onion shoots from the yard and laid them on top. "You know how to start a love letter to a possum?" he said. "Possum, O! possum . . ."

He dug in like I'd never seen anyone eat before, juice dripping off his chin while he chewed and sucked the meat. He looked like a feral beast that needed to be put down. We kept quiet until there were only bones left. "Feed the rest to the hogs," he said, handing me his plate. "They'll eat anything."

"You really got quite an operation out here," I said.

"Last-resort desperation. What was I supposed to do? *Not move in?*"

"Yeah."

"Yeah *move* in? Or yeah *not* move in? I'm asking you."

"Yeah, it was empty," I said.

"I put a camera in the toilet bowl. Maybe you've heard of me. Toilet Bowl Guy. That's why I'm up here. Get some peace and fucking quiet. I'm not ashamed. It's all happening anyways, all that piss and shit. Why can't I watch? It's not like it's not happening if I can't see it."

"True."

"People ought to be open with each other. Share what's on the inside of ourselves, you know? I'm a caring person. I like to know how a woman feels on the inside."

"You're a sensitive guy."

"Did I ask you to touch me? Don't touch me, fuck. K?"

"I didn't."

"I said, Don't!"

The noise of wind over my ears. The bending pines. I shut up and listened.

"You know, some motherfucker turned me in. That's why I'm up here. I'll figure out who it was. Soon as I finish going through all my footage. The stuff they didn't get from me. Got weeks of it, man. Months."

We were sitting around an open cooler watching a few cans of Coors float in the melted ice. I dumped a gym bag of Arnett's power tools onto the porch and started untangling cords. He told me good luck and got up to go inside. "I'm going to find Jennifer," he said. "Learn about her interior self."

I worked for a while longer on the cords, drank some beer and watched the day get hotter. The plates of bones remained on the porch. Eventually a green Jeep Wrangler with mud splashes on the sides rolled into the middle of the lot and parked with its front wheels at a cut. The man driving had some trouble getting out. His shoulders sloped under a gray suit jacket and his head, even when he looked up, seemed bowed. "Howdy," he said.

"Wesley?"

"How you know me?" He opened his hands and then closed them. "Wait." He put on his glasses. "It's you."

"I'm up here working," I said. "Finally got a job, you know." I still owed him shy of a grand.

"Working," he said, like the idea was something to consider. It was Saturday and he was wearing a tie, hadn't even loosened it. We stood there not talking, him looking around and taking it all in. Not knowing what else to do, I invited him inside for a cold drink. He nodded as if that was a possible solution.

Arnett came out the front door in army shorts and a tuxedo top. When he saw Wesley, he held out a finger of warning.

"Just came up for a smoke," Wesley said.

Arnett looked from Wesley to me and then back to him. "Told you I'm out right now," he said. "We already talked about this. Go ahead and take notes this time, if you need to. I'm not a fucking magician. Write it down. I didn't go to clown school. Write that down."

"Then remind me, please, why I'm letting you stay here."

"We talked about this already," Arnett said.

"Yes, we did, and I didn't believe you, so I thought I'd come in and see for myself."

Arnett walked back into the house, striding like he was wading through deep water toward something he was going to squeeze the life out of. Then some shouting and banging around inside.

"I think maybe you better get," I said.

"I own this heap of shit," Wesley said. "I let this convict live up here for free, under one condition. And here he goes breaking it." He crossed his arms and started scratching both elbows hard enough to leave welts. "And you," he said. "You still owe me money."

Arnett appeared in the second-story staircase window, then ducked back out of sight. He flashed past a window on the third floor. Then the fourth.

"Maybe I'll go," Wesley said. "I didn't come up here to make trouble. I just can't win right now. This place here?" he said, pointing at the inn. "I bought it for my lady. Bought it off Jack, Arnett's daddy or whatever he was. Got it for one . . . dollar . . . bill. My lady always wanted to run a breakfast-and-bed kind of thing up here. I cleared this front field myself, had chainsaws going for a month straight. I did it for her. Then one day I come home and there she is in one of our beds with another guy, some asshole with a ponytail. I asked her what she thought she was doing, and she looked at me and said, 'You've changed, Wesley.' Know what I told her?" He pointed at the invisible coward in front of him. " 'So will he.' "

He took a moment licking his teeth. I believed him but couldn't tell where I fit in his story, and that worried me.

Arnett came out onto the widow's walk, holding that same shotgun to his shoulder. Up there his hair swirled and tangled in the wind, and he yelled down that he was going to shoot himself and everybody else. He waited a moment and then called out, "Not in that order."

"Arnett!" I shouted. "Everything's cool."

"He always shows off like this," Wesley said.

Arnett pointed the gun into the air without aiming and fired. "I ain't going shitwhere!" he yelled.

"I heard you," Wesley called. He was still crouching after ducking from the shot. "You go ahead and stay right where you are."

Arnett dropped behind the walkway's railing as if to avoid return fire.

"Everybody calm the fuck down!" I said.

Wesley touched my shoulder. "Don't worry about the rest of your fee with me. We're good. Just stay up here and keep all this to yourself. Yes? And good luck." He got in his Jeep and pulled out.

Arnett came up to me shaking his head. "You realize how much information you just gave away?"

"We were just talking."

"He's a lawyer," he said. "They use everything."

"He's also your landlord."

"Is that what he said?"

"There wasn't really a problem until you started shooting."

"That's how you got to treat them," he said, looking up at where he'd been. "They'll walk all over you, bub. K?" He called over his shoulder, "Everything's clear, Jenny. Come on out, baby."

I earned my sunburn, waking early and working hard. I took long lunch breaks, drinking beer because it was good for my strength. Every now and then a couple named Eads and Terri stopped by. I watched them come and go from above. They never talked much to me, only asked where Arnett was. They seemed innocent, for potential buyers.

The sun was turning my wrinkled arm to bronze and I was almost able to get my wrist above my head.

I was beyond the trial period now but Arnett still wasn't paying me. He locked the doors at night and made me sleep on the porch. Then I lost track of the days. I hadn't seen Jennifer in a while, had only heard her voice coming from one of the bedrooms. It sounded like crying but probably wasn't.

I started working crazy hours, sun to moon. One afternoon the moon rose early and I climbed down, sat in the uncut grass and watched a tick sink itself into my leg. Arnett came out and said, "You like science? Get in here and witness this shit."

A flashlight was taped to the antler of a mount on the wall. A few oil lanterns burned in the corners. The room smelled of mildew and kerosene. Jennifer sat in a chair sipping from a milk jug, not looking at anybody. Arnett had tools and fluids spread out on the bar, around a raccoon that was still alive. He was trying to embalm it before it died. It moved so slow, focusing on every little thing, like it was amazed. He picked it up and walked it around and made it talk to Jennifer. She didn't say a word.

The next morning I woke up on the porch with her kneeling next to me, her hair making a tent over my face. "You my man, right?" she said. "I know you are. When I get back, I want him done."

She left in the truck, and I finished securing the topside of a gutter before it got too hot, then climbed down the scaffolding. Back on stable ground I rubbed my sweating palms together and sat on the edge of the porch, near my bedding.

Arnett stepped out carrying a big Styrofoam cup, his regular morning drink. He bought these at a station off 231 North and kept them in the freezer with some of the animals. He rubbed the sleep out of his eye with a fist and said, "All right, let's get to work, gotta finish before the fall."

"I been up there since seven," I told him.

"Where's Jennifer?" he said. "Where's she at?" He dumped some of the frozen green stuff from the cup into the grass and replaced it with what remained of a bottle of vodka that had been left uncapped on the table last night. He brought the cocktail over and sat beside me, took a pull, asked if I wanted some and then told me sorry, it was his. "Should've thought ahead," he said, tapping the bone between his eyebrows.

The little purple bottle was in my pocket.

He sucked at the stuff for a while, then said, "Let's talk like men." His mouth was outlined by the sharp growth of a goatee. I watched it move while he talked. "I've seen you before," he said. "Do you remember?"

My throat went dry and I couldn't swallow. A list of lies flitted through my mind.

"You were the one at Foodville," he said. "The register. Remember?" He shook the cup around, opened his mouth to where I could see his green tongue and dumped in a gulp. "Brain freeze," he said, like he'd just won something. "I remember you. You were checking her out."

The breeze blew a beech leaf over the edge of the porch. I watched it go. The humidity out here was so thick you could see it. I held a breath and tried to slow my heart.

I remembered what my boss at Foodville had told me about spotting thieves. They'll never look at you, he said. That's how you know they're about to take your shit. When they won't look at you. So I looked at Arnett and said, "Maybe, now that you mention it."

"Now that I fucking mention it," he said.

"I appreciate you hiring me," I said. "I've been needing the work."

"Really? It's not because of Jennifer?" He twinkled his fingers around like he was tickling something, then closed them into a fist. "You saying you don't like looking at her? What's wrong with her? I take issue with the fact that you don't fucking like looking at her."

"Nothing's wrong with her," I said.

"So you do like looking at her. That's what you're saying. You're here to eyeball my girl."

"Ain't nothing wrong with her. That's all I'm saying."

He nodded. "Nope. She's a tight little piece. You ought to see her upside down," he said. "Like when she can't breathe? And her face is about to bust out. Sometimes I want to see her dead, you know? That's how much I love her. Sometimes while we're crunching, I'll tell her, 'Die, you bitch, just die.'" He was making serious progress with the drink and his voice was slurring. His eyes fixed on a point ahead of us, not in the forest beyond or the yard where we sat, but something somewhere in the space between.

"What's she think about that?" I said.

"She likes it when I tell her to die. It's not my fault that's what she wants. You think it's my fault?"

"No. You really love her."

"Don't tell me who I fucking love. She'll say shit like, 'Tell me to die again.' Shit like that. And if I do it long enough, when she's about to come she'll say, 'Oh God, oh my God, I'm dying, I'm dying.'"

He took a live shotgun shell from the table, shoved it between two boards supporting the porch roof and pointed at the brass circle gleaming around the nickel hammer button. "Hit the bull's-eye," he said, and took a socket wrench and smacked it.

The blast split my ears. Splinters of wood flying.

"I'm dead! I'm dead!" He threw his hands back. The slurpee was at his feet. He picked it up, gulped again and then went around the corner to piss.

The cup stood next to me. I took the bottle out of my pocket, ears still singing and beating, unscrewed the cap, poured the solution into the drink and stirred it around with the straw, then shoved the bottle in my pocket. I'd bury it in the woods later. I walked to the edge of the yard, in case he sniffed the drink, and looked down over the world.

Some other leaf was sailing around out there. But the more I stared at it, the more it looked like a small hole, a little puncture wound in the sky. What if there was an entire world behind the surface of this one? A darker place made of all the things we hide?

He came back, picked up the cup and drained it, hissed like a match getting doused, went up the porch steps and took a seat at the table. "I Inadulterated," he said, pulling out a pack of cigarettes. "Smooth morning time." He ran his fingers through his hair and tossed his head a few times like he had water in his ears. "Over there," he said. "The fuck is that?"

It was the sound of an engine. "I'll check it out," I told him.

The noise of tires on shale rose from the bottom of the hollow. Jennifer's truck was moving up the access road, trailing a dust cloud.

He leaned back in the chair. "Think I need to lie down."

"Somebody's coming," I said.

"Oh yeah? What other secrets you want to let me in on?"

Arnett looked like he'd become very heavy. He got out of the chair and lay on his back on the boards. The truck was making steady progress. With her shades on, Jennifer sat in the cab clutching the wheel, and it looked like she was grooving. Arnett lay next to the plates of possum bones, his hand across his middle as it rose and fell.

The grass out back between the inn and the barn was knee high. It sounded like a breath in the breeze. The worn boards of the barn had collapsed into some kind of fencing, and that's where the pigs and dogs were waiting. Two bungee cords held the gate shut, and they hung back against the fence when I unlatched them. The hogs were squealing and bouncing, the hounds slinking behind them and starting into an open cry when I pushed the gate door, and they raced out, snatching and slavering at one another. I'd heard of pigs eating their own farmers, and they ran away from the barn like they knew what they were supposed to do.

I met the truck partways down and climbed in. "Turn around," I told her. "*Now.*"

"You get it done?"

"I did what you said."

She drove up to the edge of the lot to turn around. I looked at the porch but couldn't make out whether Arnett was there or not. "Keep turning," I said. "Keep going."

"Let's just check." She yanked the emergency brake. "See how capable you really are."

"He was down the last I saw. There's nothing else we can do. Let's please get the fuck away from here."

She started back down the access and my hands shook as I gripped my knees, from nerves and the road rattling us. She took a longneck from her purse. Trees blended green in the window behind her. She eased the bottle between my legs with fingers around the top of it, but I couldn't appreciate the sight. "I can't right now," I said.

"You better."

I turned it up to my mouth and it foamed onto my shirt. She was right, it was calming, so I began telling her how it all went down. She stood on the brake and we side-tailed in the gravel. "So he's alive," she said. "You fucked up a perfectly easy thing."

I looked out my window and took another swig.

She got out, came around to open my door and told me to get out. I set the bottle on the floorboard and stepped down just as she swung at me in the road. I jumped back and she went reeling from the miss, tripping and rolling into the ditch. I stood over her. "It might be working," I said. "He drank the stuff. He did that. We need to get going."

"We need to stay right here." She got up and went back to the truck and brought out a handle of bourbon. Some was already gone.

"Don't point that at me."

"Let's get a blanket," she said. "Go into the woods and hide out. I mean, camp. We don't got a thing to hide because we didn't do anything. We didn't run. Only people who run are the people that did something." She left the bottle on the bench seat, put a foot on the rear wheel and hopped into the bed.

While she was gathering her stuff, I unscrewed the cap and poured warm whiskey down my throat. It burned my stomach. I took another drink for good luck. What was I worried about? Things had gone perfect. I gave a guy what he asked for. I didn't have to explain shit to anybody. It was hot out and he drank too much. That same old story.

The truck didn't have a blanket, only a tarp. We hiked it far back in the woods, spread it out and started drinking properly in our nice little nest, all leaves and sticks and plastic. We drank until Nitro Mountain's light started glowing somewhere behind us.

"It's getting dark," I said.

"It already did that," she said.

I got up and walked over to a tree for a piss and then a puke. "We gotta go."

"I'm sorry I didn't think you gave it to him," she said. She was on her knees and brushing off the tarp, a black square in the thicket. She patted the place beside her. Somehow I made it there and we finished the bottle. "Next what we do is wait and see what happens and keep quiet," she said. "But enough of that for now. There's one more thing I need."

She rolled into a position I'd never seen before. She stuck her backside up, clutching her ass and spreading it and begging to get hit. "All this, all yours. Think of our years together," she said. "Or months or whatever. All I wanted was."

Afraid I'd be done in her before she felt it, I took her by the ribs with my good hand and she looked over her shoulder. "Hit me," she said. "Come on."

The light behind us colored my fist. Her hair went flying and her face went down and I kept hitting her and hitting her until she stopped talking.

No sun yet. But it was warm out and the woods were beginning to brighten. My body was covered in chiggers and ticks. I pulled up my pants leg and it looked like I had scales. Her swollen face was a mound of putty painted in generous dark layers. Bruises from my own hands dotted her neck and arms and side and legs. Marks of my own teeth on top of the hogs'. The pain of light fired into my temple like a nail gun. I must've gotten up and then fallen down, because when I woke up again I was in the truck riding beside her.

"Get out," she said. "We're here."

I saw where we were: my parents' house. Her face looked even worse. "You need to get help," I said.

"We can't be seen together."

"Where you going to go?"

"Give me forty bucks," she said. "I'll get a room at the Knight's Inn and we can meet there later."

I handed her two twenties from my wallet.

———

The kitchen smelled like burnt toast. I didn't see Mom at first, even though she was sitting right there at the table. It seemed like she'd been waiting for this moment and now here it was and she didn't know what to say.

"Foodville's been calling for you," she said. "Where've you been?"

"I moved out like you told me to."

"I told you nothing of the sort," she said.

"I got another job. You can't yell at me anymore."

"I never yell at you. Are you all right? Look at you."

"Fuck Foodville. They can go fuck themselves. I do what I want. They should've figured that out by now. You too."

"My boy," she said. "Please sit down."

I opened the fridge and she told me to take what I wanted. I looked in, then punched the door shut. "I don't want any of that," I said.

Dad moved into the kitchen doorway, gripping his lower back. "He been sleeping with that slut," he said, talking to Mom but looking at me. "That's where he been. Can't you smell it on him?"

Mom tried stopping me but she couldn't. She cried for me to quit. I had pushed my father to the floor and he was lying there yelling.

"After everything we done give you," he said.

"You call this everything?" I stepped over him into the living room. "Take a look around." He wouldn't, so I helped him. "This lamp," I said, and threw it. "This coffee table," I said, and dumped it.

"What do you want?" my mother said. "You're my boy. What do you want? I'll do anything."

She was the only one in our little world holding shit together, and I couldn't face her. "Throw it all away," I said. "Flush it."

"I won't let you," she cried.

Dad lay there in the mess I'd made. "If I get up I'll kill your ass," he said.

"That's exactly your problem," I said. "You can't."

"I sure will."

"Let me help you." I pulled him by the arm and dragged him around the room. He seemed so small, like a toy dad. Mom was begging. When I realized he actually couldn't get up, I let him go.

"Call the cops," he told my mom.

I could see his heart hammering in his chest. It was a crazy hammer. "What?" I said. "For me not kicking your ass? Make sure you hide your weed before they get here."

I slammed the front door so hard the storm glass fell out and shattered on the front stoop. The dealer boy stood in his yard and watched me walk down the driveway. I sensed his attention. Down the road a ways I figured he'd stopped staring, but when I turned around he was still there.

I walked for miles through fields and scrub forest to the Knight's Inn. A lot of it was creek land, and my pants were soaked by the time I got there. A truck was parked between two yellow lines on the new asphalt; it wasn't hers. A few sedans were lined up in front of other rooms. I didn't want to ask or knock or let anybody notice me, so I went over to the wooden fence around the dumpsters, pushed the chained doors apart and squeezed through.

I crouched against the slats, sweat stinging my eyes. The sun was getting high, no shade anywhere. A couple cars came. In one of the dumpsters I found a pizza box and ate the crusts. I reconsidered knocking on some doors but decided not to listen to myself anymore. When I heard another car turning in, I peeked out and watched a guy park. He walked up and knocked on a door. It opened and he went in. I wiped my face with my shirt, then held it over my nose and mouth to keep out the stench of baking garbage. I waited for so long before the guy came out with a girl. They stood around the hood of his car, smoking and talking, just a couple that had nothing to do with me.

The sun touched the treetops and I hitched a ride out of town with a man who asked if I believed in aliens. When I said I didn't know, he unwrapped a stick of gum, folded it into his mouth and chewed it for a while before swallowing it.

"Everybody says yes or no," he said.

"Everybody but me," I said. When we got to the foot of Nitro I told him to drop me off.

"Only if you say yes or no," he said.

"I already told you."

He slowed onto the shoulder and we rolled to a stop. "That's what I thought," he said. "No *yes*, no *no*."

I took the woods. Each time I dropped into a hollow I lost my directions and got turned around. At a rocky overhang with cool dirt beneath it, I lay down and fell asleep. When I woke up it was dark as a rat snake.

Quartz jutted along a ridge like broken spine and I followed it up to the inn. Over the front field, the clouds smeared the sky and passed beneath a cut of moon heading west. A hallway light was on. No police tape anywhere.

He wasn't on the porch where I'd left him. But the plates of possum bones were.

In the barroom, I turned on the lights and lit the place up. I searched under the tables and behind the bar and in the kitchen but nobody was there, so I went to the next floor up and walked down the long hallway, every single door wide open, and realized I could go into whichever room I wanted. It was a strange feeling, such freedom. I went to the door at the end of the hall. Arnett's bedroom. A rifle lay across the sheets, but otherwise there was nothing except the same dead animals.

Hearing something downstairs, I grabbed the rifle, went back down to the bar and shut out the lights, took a stool and steadied the rifle in my lap. Listening. I thought to check for a bullet in the chamber and flicked a lighter at it. I heard footsteps outside in the grass. Then a bright beam shot through a slit in the blinds. Then the footsteps again, now on the porch boards.

In the voice of someone who knew what he was doing, who was supposed to be here, I said, "Who is it?"

I almost believed it was just Wesley coming to check on things. When he stepped inside, I'd show him the rifle and explain that I was guarding his place. I'd tell him to sit down, have a beer, the tap's open. Draw you one and get a seat. He would ask me what was wrong. He'd say I didn't look like the kind of guy to hurt anybody. Then Jennifer would walk into the room and say, He's not.

Do you know what growing up means? It means learning to beat a woman. Trying to kill a man. Posting up at a worn-out palace with a loaded gun and waiting to deal with the consequences of what you've done.

2

The oak trees in the center of Bordon turn silver in the wind. Streetlamps blink on as another thunderstorm flashes the horizon. The pawnshop that used to be the antique shop along the square is closing; a shirtless man pulls in the sidewalk chalkboard, its slogan, *You Lost It We Got It,* smearing and running. The stoplight swings, turns red and a car runs right through it as the librarian watches, standing there by a shelf of free books. She stomps the wheel-lock open and rolls the cart back inside. A slinking cat pours off the top of a trash can and runs into the street, the same car missing it by inches.

Carol drives north up 231. Leaving the town limits, she glances over and spots a pack of hounds standing in the field. A practice hunt, this time of year. The hunter has parked his Tacoma on the shoulder. He drops the tailgate, opens the cage and calls for them with a two-fingered whistle when she steers around him. Rain slashes the road, then her windshield. A few miles farther a lane peels off to the left with a row of low-income ranch houses sinking into the earth. The last one is hers. She pulls into the driveway, gets out, eyes heavenward, and asks where her boy went off to this time.

A turkey vulture glides over her house in the oncoming gale and then it's gone, pulling more clouds and rain along behind it. "An omen," she says out loud. Lightning flares, capturing each iridescent drop in its moment of falling. She remembers summer storms, but none like this.

The vulture leaves Carol below, slipping upward in a warm whipstream over pastures and forests and fields toward the ridge, the foothills dipping and rising and rolling, streams and train tracks crossing and racing one another, flying higher until the town of Bordon is a spot of mold in the earth's green carpeting.

The vulture shelters in a tree-hole before the storm crashes in. Finally, with the sky opening, the rain easing, it flies again. Sensing something at the top of the ridge, it circles, finds a towering dead pine and takes roost in the bare branches. A figure in the woods below. The bird turns its head, helmeted in red scalded scar-flesh, toward the scent of carrion.

✕◇✕

Inside Larry's Hickory Honky Tonk, Jones rests an elbow along the copper bar. He's got Hank moaning through the old cathedral-shaped jukebox. *When tears come down, like falling rain.* Quarters bulge out his pants pocket and he's patting them to the beat of the song. It's happy hour, not late at all, but outside the rain's pouring down. *You'll toss around, and call my name.* Water gushes over the back windows. Out there, Larry has a makeshift marina, the dock made from planks and barrels, enough space for a couple bass boats. There's also a spot for the pontoon he used to own; it sat in the water and served as the outdoor stage that Jones and his band used to play on. They packed this place during the summer months. But that's not the deal anymore. Tonight the listening room's empty, and it's a goddamn shame—everybody staying home because of a little flash flood warning. Back in the day, folks braved tornadoes to hear Jones Young play.

The tour with Marshall Mac ended on a low note, the band hungry and tired, Jones doing all the driving. After they'd played their last gig in Ohio, he drove Jerry and Matt back to their girlfriends' houses in central Virginia and decided to take his time getting back south to Ashland, his old home place. He traveled around for a few days in the Econoline, gigging at dives to prove to himself he could still do it. That's what he did all through high school. And compared to the big rooms he opened for Marshall Mac in, it's what he prefers. The van's paid off and he's been writing his own songs. They're good, people say. About to finish another one soon. Who needs a band anyway?

"What're you drinking?" Larry says.

Jones goes over and thumbs more quarters into the jukebox. "Dickel."

"Come on, don't start that. Tell me what you want." Larry points to the line of craft beers on draft. He stopped serving liquor here because of the noise it caused. Somebody would be onstage, and then here comes some loudmouth, half a bottle deep and thinking it's his or her turn with the mic. The Hickory's main course now is music, beer for a side. He'll throw together a few burgers too.

"It's raining," Jones says. "Let me bring in my whiskey. It won't cost you nothing. Nobody's showing up tonight, man."

"Must've been too long of a tour for you." Larry turns his head and studies the rain, like this is something he might make sense of. Then he pats the bar with his left hand, the one that's missing its peace fingers.

"*Too* long," Jones says. "Marshall Mac and the Fuck-You-Tees."

"How was Nashville? You make any contacts?" Larry's always getting at Jones about keeping up with the business side. He lost his two fingers in the line of duty, he claims, and soon after, when he realized he'd never be able to play guitar again, he left the force and started the Honky Tonk. Wanted to put his money back into something he loved. Give local and touring musicians a place to play. At the Hickory's first show, when he heard young

Jones stumbling through Tony Rice's "Old Train," he came up to him afterward and said he was a boy he could teach to pick like he used to, if Jones'd just listen to him for a minute.

"Hell no, I didn't make any *contacts*," Jones says. "Some of the band was still trying to figure out the arrangements. There we were, onstage, looking like a bunch of assholes. That's how Nashville was."

Larry turns his back, takes a glass and pulls beer into it. "You'll like this one. Unfiltered IPA. Almost strong as that stuff you like."

"This shit hurts me," Jones says, taking the cloudy pint.

"I was expecting your band to be with you."

"The last bass player we had sucked worse than the one with the broken arm."

"You had a broken-arm bass player?" Larry says. "Now that's country music."

"It was, man. I hated letting him go. Jerry replaced him with a jazz guy who wouldn't quit walking the neck—bompa-bompa, bompa-bompa—and he had this fretless stick-bass thing that sounded like a synth. And worse, his intonation was haywire. It was embarrassing. I really started missing that first guy."

"What's his name?"

"Leon. Just some boy from Bordon, you wouldn't know him. Dude was in trouble, man. He couldn't hardly even think straight. Don't know how he played a lick, and that arm was the least of his problems. But I liked him."

"Your worst picker's as good as the band will ever get. That's what your dad used to say."

"I know it."

"He'd be proud of what you're doing."

"Maybe."

"He believed in you, Jones. And he was right about most things."

"I don't feel like talking about him." Jones slugs the rest of the thick brew. "This shit's awful."

"All right," Larry says. "Bring your whiskey in."

Jones runs out to the van, hoofing through puddles in his cowboy boots, and comes back soaking wet and carrying a tall bottle of tan-label sour mash. Larry sets out a taster and Jones pours a jigger. "To my father." He lifts it up and waits for a toast.

"Shoot, now. There you go with that talk." Larry brings out another taster and pours himself one. "To your father."

They clink and drink. The whiskey sizzles the tip of Jones's tongue, and he dumps the rest down.

"I'm going to put this bottle back here and regulate your intake," Larry says. "That all right?"

"Yeah, just give me one more pour before you do."

"So you're going solo?"

"Till I find some guys who fit my playing."

"Pretty hard around here."

"Maybe it'll give me a chance to try out some new songs," Jones says.

"Originals, that's what the agents want." Larry scoops some ice, drops it into Jones's glass and pours him another one.

"Right, the fucking agents." Jones tips the glass up. "Do me a favor, no more ice."

"I'm excited to see how it goes for you, Jones, just you and your guitar. I think it could be good. Strip it down, you know."

"I'm working on a new song."

"Glad to hear it. You sleeping in your van?"

"No," Jones says. "Yes."

"You know there's an empty room at my house."

Jones pushes his glass out and Larry gives him a generous vertical turn of the bottle. "Last one."

Jones shoots the big drink down his throat and drops the glass back onto the bar. This should be a good evening at the Hickory.

Nobody here to impress except Larry—good luck with that—so why not have a few pops before the set. "I appreciate it," he says.

"What're you doing tomorrow? You got anything booked?"

"Did."

"I got the Jags in here tomorrow night. You want to open? It'd be only for tips. But hell, far as tips go, you can play happy hour every day this week if you want to."

"Might, might not. Thanks, though. I just feel like bumming around a little bit more. Probably go see Natalie, since I'm officially back in town."

That's his ex-wife, who lives down the road. Larry shakes his head. "She ain't been doing well."

"Drinking," Jones says. "Messing around every night. And, let me guess. Coming over here during shows and making a racket. That song wrote *me*."

"Try not to start nothing if you see her. Every time she comes in here she's hellfire."

"I'm just going to swing by and check on her, see what's up. Well, that and she's still got my guitar case. If she's drinking that much, I better get it before she burns it to ashes or something."

The wind sends the branch of a poplar scraping across the side window, which creaks and cracks and then breaks. "There she goes," Larry says.

"There she goes again," Jones says.

"I got to take care of that branch tomorrow before it kills the tree."

Larry's good at getting shit done. Can't not be busy. He even fronted the money for Jones's first demo. About half the CDs are still behind the register in cardboard boxes. And they're not really all that bad. Ask any of the thirty-three dopes who bought one.

Jones gets up, goes behind the bar and grabs the bottle. "Let's do one more. You and me."

The whiskey glugs from the long-barreled neck into his glass. Jones sets it down in front of him, points at it and says, "Who you think you looking at?" He turns to Larry. "You gonna let this guy talk to me like that?"

"What's he saying?"

"He says I'm too chicken to drink him. He's sitting right here calling me names. He don't even know me." Jones stands up, adjusts his belt and sits back down. "And I just heard him say something about my mama."

"Ah, shit." Larry rubs his eyes.

"You know what I'm about to do to you?" Jones asks the glass. "I'm about to suck your ass *down*."

Larry walks over, opens the front door and leans out for some air. Jones tips the bottle up to his mouth, pulls it away, looks around, then takes it up once more and screws on the cap.

"I saw that," Larry says.

"Just making sure I can take care of his friends before I start dealing with him."

"You need some backup?"

"Might," Jones says. "Yeah, shit. I'm down and they're kicking me."

Larry comes over and drinks the rest of it. Jones unscrews the bottle and pours another short one. "This guy's been talking shit too."

The uneven floor around Jones's stool allows him to rock along to the music. He's only thirty but has real sympathy for these old songs. He looks into his drink. *Staring through a glass of bourbon straight.* He grabs a bleach-white napkin from a chrome box on the counter, writes that thought down and puts it in the back pocket of his jeans. "My next song's about nobody but you," he says to his drink.

"Y'all make up that fast?"

"We just had a misunderstanding is all. Ain't that right, Mr. Dickel?" His foot slips off the footrest and hits his Gibson leaning against the bar, knocking it to the floor. All the strings ringing out.

"Hell," Larry says. "That's the one thing your daddy left you. If you ain't going to play it, put it up."

"She's got the case."

"Who?"

"Natalie. I just told you. I'll play it when everybody shows up."

"Ain't nobody showing up tonight, Jones."

"You'll see." He picks up his guitar and sets it across his lap. He drains the drink, flips the guitar upright and hits a big A. It's almost in tune with the song that's playing, so he starts banging away and singing along, "Won't you come to my arms, sweet darling, and stay?"

"I know the answer to that question," Larry says. He puts the bottle out of sight, pushes some numbers on the register and rings him up. "Five bucks."

Jones wipes his chin, strums harder and finishes, "The hell you trying to pull?" He puts his guitar down, goes behind the bar, stumbles over the rubber floor mat, grabs the bottle from below the register and carries it back to his stool.

"Don't," Larry says.

With the bottle uncapped in his hand, Jones blinks at him. "I just had an idea: Fuck no."

"Five bucks. Or quit drinking now."

"Look here," Jones says. "I got a new song. Want to hear it?"

"No."

"That's what it's called!"

"Listen," Larry says, "I can't just have you drinking like this. And then acting like this."

"*You* listen. I been drinking, okay?"

"*One* thing we can agree on."

"So we're in agreement. Good. I been drinking because I ain't been playing."

"Ain't been playing because you been drinking."

"I ain't been playing because nobody's here. Which is why I been drinking. Which is your fault. So. Here's to me, because nobody's like me and nobody likes me." He takes a long pull from the bottle.

The music stops, and Jones goes over to the jukebox.

"You better come back to my place," Larry says.

"I ain't going nowhere," Jones says, "and I ain't never coming back." He sways to his seat.

Larry's holding the bottle. "Now I'm not kidding."

"Well, why didn't you say so?" Jones blinks at him again.

"*Been* saying so."

"Fine," Jones says. "Let's clean things up and head back to your place."

"Sounds good. You don't mind sleeping in the living room, do you? Sharon's been staying with me and we like to keep the upstairs to ourselves."

"You love her yet?"

"Yeah. Told her, too." He puts the bottle back down.

Jones can tell he's about to get a story out of this old soft-heart. He takes out the napkin again and flattens it in front of him.

"I'd like to marry her," Larry says. "If she'll let me. Ain't asked her yet, though."

Jones stops the pen on the paper and looks up at him. "Bullshit. Don't lie."

"No shit. None at all."

"So when you gonna ask? You got a band to play the wedding yet? I'll give you a bargain."

"We'll talk tomorrow," Larry says. "When you're sober."

"Since when was I sober tomorrow?"

Somebody's banging on the front door and they both look over their shoulders. A lady's standing outside with her hands cupped around her face, nose pressed to the glass and long, wet hair draping down.

Larry opens the door. "Come in out the rain, sweetheart."

"Y'all still serving?" She leaves a puddle where she stands.

"Hell yeah," Jones says.

"Not that guy," Larry says, and points at Jones. "But honey, if you need something."

Her face is thin and flushed, and she has a black eye and a busted bottom lip. The rain runs the blood down her chin in a line of pink watercolor.

Jones recognizes her. Where from?

She takes the stool next to him without even a glance. "Give me a Bud Light." She pulls a napkin and dabs her lip. Larry levers off the cap and puts it in front of her. Jones lifts his glass. "To the rain," he says. He keeps his eyes on hers and gets hers on his. "To the wetness."

"Shit," Larry says.

"So are you playing or what?" she says to Jones. If she smiles, her lips will bleed again.

"I am."

"I don't have nothing for a tip," she says.

"Quit it. Don't even start. You got *great* tips."

She looks at them and has a swig, downing half the bottle. "I'd love to hear some music." She points at the stage. "Get up there and pick a little."

Like that, from one pull, she's a different person, telling Jones what to do. And Jones is under her spell. Larry shakes his head.

"I'll play you something," Jones says. "Is that why you came out? To hear me?"

"No," she says. "Well, yeah, but not really."

"Good enough."

"My boyfriend, he did this to me last night." She points at her face with the bottle. "I had to move out here to the Lakewood so he couldn't find me."

"Let's get this straight," Jones says. "Did you come to hear me or not?"

"I don't even know who you are."

"Wish I could say the same for you."

"Enough, Jones," Larry says.

"Leon," Jones says. "That's who you're talking about."

"Wait, now," she says. "How do you . . . Wait, you're Jones Young."

"At your mercy."

"This ain't all he did to me," she says. "He did something real bad to my boyfriend too."

"Thought you said Leon was your boyfriend," Larry says.

"Well, he was."

"Okay," Jones says. "So what'd your boyfriend do to your boyfriend?" He lifts his eyebrows at Larry, who nods. Jones unscrews the bottle and offers it to her. She takes it.

"See, my other boyfriend, Leon, was like freaked out by—anyway. Me and Leon used to be together. We started—is this being embarrassing?—we started sleeping together again."

"Together again," Jones sings.

"While I was still living with the other one." She looks around. "I shouldn't be telling y'all this."

"Drink a little bit more," Jones says.

"You'll feel better," Larry says.

"Will you drink with me?" she says. "I'm scared of being alone right now."

She scoots close to Jones and he can smell her perfume, a

cheap flower scent cut with vanilla. Her knee touches his and makes his balls tighten. "I'll drink with you," he says.

"So Leon starts getting these ideas? This crazy shit. That he wants to, like, kill Arnett."

"Arnett was the other boyfriend?" Larry puts both hands on the bar and lowers his head.

"Normal breakup stuff," Jones says. "Only natural."

"He was serious," Jennifer says. "I wasn't about to get mixed up in any of that. I don't want murder on my soul."

Jones jots down a line on the napkin and puts it back in his pocket. "I remember what Leon was like on tour," he says. "I could never tell what that guy was thinking. But come on, there's no chance in hell he was serious about that."

"Hush up," Larry says. "Let the girl talk."

"Problem is," Jennifer says, "I think he did it."

"How do you know this?" Larry says.

"I just have this tingle. A very bad little tingle."

"You're going on a tingle?" Larry says.

"Nothing wrong with that," Jones says. "I've tingled before and I'm not afraid to tingle again."

"I ain't shitting you," Jennifer says. "He was always talking about doing it. And now I don't know where he is. He might still be up there."

"Up where?" Larry says.

She tosses her hand over her head and points straight up. "Nitro."

"Jack's place?" Larry says.

"Arnett's Jack's son," Jennifer says. "Or was. Or somebody's."

"I know that. Last time I saw him he was about eighteen, wearing shorts made of chicken-feed bags. Just *covered* in scabies. I went up there to check on a Child Protective Services call. To see what Jack was doing. That's how I got this." He holds up his bad hand as if taking some warped oath.

"Now you done it," Jones says to Jennifer. "Getting him started back on the old cop stuff. That's exactly what gets him every time. Who's doing what-where-when. Next he'll start into how bad us young folks are. Just listen. He's given me the whole speech before. Careful—you'll get it too."

"Son of a bitch caught me with shot-spray out in the woods. 'Sorry, didn't mean to,' he says, while I'm kneeling there bleeding in the fucking leaves. Then defends himself, successfully, saying he was hunting. Season was open, I'll give him that. And I didn't have a warrant to be on his land, true, not yet. Court found him innocent. And he still ran. Don't know where he went. Nobody does. I been wondering lately what's happening on that mountain."

"I think that's where Leon is," she says. "Something real fucked's going down up there."

"Turner," Larry says. "He thinks as much, too."

"Oh, Jesus," Jones says. "Now we gotta bring Turner into this?"

They'd come on the force around the same time. Turner stayed on after Larry left, then ended up getting fired for fighting with some new cops who, in Larry's humble opinion, are a bunch of horse's asses.

"I bet that's where Leon is," she says.

"So what you're saying," Larry says, "is you don't know where he's at but you bet you do. Is it Jack's spot?"

"Up on Nitro," she says. "At the Lookout."

"That's that place," Larry says. "Goddamn. I thought Wesley owned it by now."

"Anyway," she says, "Leon's either there or somewhere else on the ridge."

"East Ridge?" Larry says.

"Yeah. That backside."

"You talking about Wesley the lawyer?" Jones says. "I know

that guy. Man's a ringleader. Hey girl, keep talking about the backside."

"I wouldn't go up there right now for nothing," Jennifer says.

"I would." Jones snaps his fingers.

"You need a tongue scrubbing," Larry says.

"I told Leon to talk to Wesley," Jones says, "when he was dealing with his court shit."

Color leaves her face and she bends over the bar, touches her nose to the copper and straightens up. "I'm sick of thinking about it. Maybe it didn't happen at all. It might not've happened. Play me a song, Jones."

"There you go," Jones says. He's going to sing his new song, and that normally wouldn't shake him. He can't think why it does.

"I tell you, though," she says, "remembering what he said he was going to do to Arnett . . ."

"It's all right," Jones says. "*You're* all right. You deserve a song."

"Just make it sad."

"I'm sure he's got that covered." Larry's staring at something only he can see, working the muscle in his jaw, not even in the room with them anymore.

Jones takes his guitar and weaves toward the stage. Leon. Crazy old Leon. "Larry, unplug the jukebox," Jones says. "She's lonesome. And Jones Young is in the building."

Awake and asleep, he says, "Why were you ever up there with any of those dudes?"

"Same reason I'm with you."

———

Daylight splinters into the room, across Jennifer's sleeping face. The motel sheets are clean and starched. Jones sits up and the rush of blood pounds his head. He keeps an eye closed, looks over the side of the bed for his guitar. It's right there. No case, but there. That's good.

And he's still alive. That's good, too.

He gets up and steps into his jeans. His heart's beating like it's trying to get loose. He looks around for his hat. Must've left it at the Hickory. He'll stop by for it before going to Natalie's to grab the case. He sits on the chair in the corner, slips a menthol cigarette from the pack that's sticking out of Jennifer's pleather purse and blows smoke at the sealed window, catching a line of morning light.

How she looks right now makes Jones want to stay. But that isn't going to happen. He gathers his stale socks and pulls them over his feet. Her body beneath the white sheet makes a snowy mountain range. She stirs, shifting the topography. Last night he woke up in her arms. It felt like dreaming. Her fingers on his skin. He takes the napkin from his back pocket and writes another line to what he hopes is a song. There's the bottle next to the coffee pot, uncapped with a few inches left. He gets up, the cigarette in his mouth, takes the bottle in his right hand and the guitar in his left and manages the doorknob with two fingers.

Streams of dirty water sparkle across the blacktop. The bright day makes him squint. It'd look like he was grinning, if someone were watching right now.

Jones can still smell her in his mustache. The Econoline's taking up two spaces at the far end of the lot. He doesn't recall much about driving here last night, but the way it's sitting there crooked tells him enough. He does remember she was on him the second he opened the door, pulling at him, begging, and he was worried that after all the whiskey he'd be a cooked noodle and she wouldn't have any fun. But her mouth sobered him up pretty good. Her lips were bleeding a little and that made the kissing slick. Forgetting her will take some time, he knows that. And that whole Leon thing. What the hell? He can understand why Leon was willing to kill for her. Or at least talk about it. She has that kind of power. Jones doesn't blame him for a minute.

※◇※

Arnett remembers his mother planting tomatoes outside his open bedroom window, and Jack, his uncle-dad, coming back from the shed carrying the moldy leg of a deer, its hoof dragging behind him and making a broken line in the dust. The hounds had brought it out of the woods. His mother was wearing a straw sunhat. Arnett could see him coming up behind her. Still can.

Jack was, by blood, Arnett's uncle. The last time they talked was maybe ten years ago, right before he ran off after shooting that cop, and Arnett wouldn't be surprised if Jack was living like a fool bum somewhere, thinking he was still in trouble. Jack the Uncle. Stupid-ass uncle-dad.

Arnett's real father died on a blast-mining job before they even had the explosives in place and is now just a soiled spot trapped in the tunnels of his son's mind. He was cutting away coalbed when the mountain flexed. And that was it. Gone. Buried beneath the hills of Watts, Kentucky, where they were all living at the time.

Arnett never did any mining, no fucking thank you, he ain't about all that. If you asked him who he's closer in kin with, he'd have to say Jack.

After his father's death, Jack married his mother and brought them to the outskirts of Bordon, where he bought some land with the money paid to compensate the loss of his brother, his new wife's old husband, on top of the hill he'd climbed when he first arrived, which was in fact a mountain—what's a few extra feet?—and nobody much stepped foot on it. He'd bought it for cheap from the coal company; they were damn happy to wash their hands of all potential lawsuits and calm the family down. Motivated by delusions of prosperity, he began building a house up there, a kind of fortressed inn he called the Lookout.

And that's the issue with Wesley. He's always going on about how *I built this house for my love, I built it with my bare dick.* No he didn't. Arnett's uncle-dad did. And then, when Jack split, Arnett tried selling some of his corn liquor and got busted. Go figure. He got arrested for public intoxication every single time he went into town. So he hired Wesley for all the court dates and ended up owing him twelve grand. He didn't have five bucks on him, or anywhere else, so he gave that asshole the inn.

Wesley paid the back taxes and started fixing the place up for his wife, who turned out to be a bitch, and once they separated he began relying on substances provided him by clients who couldn't otherwise pay his fees. He invited Arnett back to the Lookout in hopes of turning it into a play-palace—a buffet of whores and hooch, the bar loaded with every yellow beer available and barrels of bourbon left over from local distilleries that wanted in on the fun. Arnett dreamed of parties lasting for days, women tied up and drooling. He was supposed to make this happen. But look at him now. Writhing from what that little motherfucker drank him with.

He can still see Jack grabbing his mom that day and saying, "Do you not hear me?" He saw her sunhat fall off and ran outside to help her, but Jack was beating her with the deer leg. He remembers seeing that torn-open paper packet of seeds lying in the dirt, and Jack standing over her. It all makes him step outside his body now and see himself standing like that over Leon.

Maybe he can't even help it.

The grass was still wet with dew when he snuck around the inn. He'd been self-medicating in the barn with splo for at least twenty-four hours—he was so fucked up it was hard to tell. But he did know it was still dark out when he crept onto the porch with a flashlight to see who the hell was in his house.

He prayed it was who he thought it was. Self-defense, motherfucker. And bingo. The kid was too scared to even try to shoot. Arnett lifted the rifle from his arms and invited him outside. "I just wanna show you something," he said.

Now there's stains splattered all over his shirt from the business he just finished. It's raining off and on. The pain in his stomach makes him lash his arms across his middle until he folds, almost like he's laughing, and comes back up to say, "Might the problem with this predicament be irreversible? I think not. Then stand straight up, you cracker fuck."

Water forms at the lower rims of his eyelids. Weak tear ducts, his mother used to say, so he always carries a handkerchief and never lets anybody see him wiping away the unintentional weeping. It's the most embarrassing thing he could've imagined, tears coming from nowhere. They never meant sadness; he doesn't believe he's ever felt much of that. Like the time Jennifer, gone most of the day, came home from the mall all done up and asked if he'd missed her, and he said, I don't know what that means. She was the only one to have ever seen the eye fluids, and she even gave him a reason for it. When you get scared, she said. When you get cold, when you get angry, when you get drunk. That's when you cry. It's not crying, he told her, and then knocked her down.

Better off without that bitch.

He pulls out the handkerchief and dabs at his face. The hickory-handled shovel lies at his feet. Fog's rising out of the valleys and the clouds are low. The sun breaks through for a moment, a psychotic lamp without location. He looks out over the rutted lot, across the eastern foothills toward where corpse-like cattle sometimes nibble. The porch boards crack and squeak when he goes back up to get a better view of things. He grabs the binoculars off the table and scans South Hill and other possible sight points on the access. A chickenhawk screams somewhere in the trees. Nobody saw nothing. He tosses the binoculars down into the grass and they land beside Leon, who's lying facedown in the trampled mud. Wind flicking his hair.

He moves carefully down the stairs, bends over to grab the shovel and retches. Slugs of blood and bile spatter the ground. With the handkerchief he wipes his mouth and eyes and walks over to Leon. A dark puddle has leaked out of the boy's head. "You feeling any better?" he says.

It's amazing how much blood can be in a person's head. It's caking Leon's hair. "Isn't that something." He whistles. "You broke, huncher."

He walks over to the shed in the side yard for more medicine. The door opens soundlessly on its truck-tire hinges, then closes on its own behind him. In the dark dirt-floored room he grabs a fruit jar of cloudy splo from a lower shelf and screws off the lid. Strips and spots of daylight shoot through the walls of warped wood into the dankness crammed with old gasoline cans, files worn smooth, chainsaw lube spilled and never cleaned up, mouse shit and dead camel crickets. An ancient possum turd in the corner half stamped by a boot toe. You can see the berry seeds in it. He closes his eyes, inhales and then takes a mouthful. Air wheezes out through his nose while he holds in the fire just like his uncle taught him. Let it fill your face till your head explodes. Why you think they call it splo, son? Don't swallow till you think you're about to die. While he's standing there with his eyes closed and his mouth full, he hears something. He swallows, glances around, kicks the door open and spots the intruder in the light that pours in. A little field mouse hiding in the corner, paws in prayer.

"Just you in here?" Arnett says. He sets the jar on the shelf, takes the handkerchief from his back pocket and wipes his eyes. "Your humility reeks," he says, then takes a gulp like the stuff was just water, holds the jar away, coughing, finishes it and throws it at the mouse, the glass smashing against the two-by-four sill. The mouse disappears.

Broad pain warms Arnett's gut. It's better than the sharp stabbing that's been there. Whatever that shit was Leon drank him with—best to stay drunk now until it fades.

Leon's still lying where Arnett brained him. Better clean this shit up. Make it so it never happened. He takes a cigarette from his shirt pocket, lights it and listens to the tobacco burn. Nothing's wrong, right? He looks south, down to the snaking East Ridge. An unmarked piece of stone down there: his mother.

Elephants, Wesley once told him, show more respect to their blood than that.

"You'll join her when it gets dark," he tells Leon, then drops the cigarette into the blood and it hisses. He picks up the shovel. "This ain't out of respect. It's just I got some work to do."

But he can still sense something. It smells like somebody's watching. He stands there long enough for his shadow to shift an inch across the mud. An engine whines somewhere down on 231. Wheat grass in the pasture below waves like water from a gust of wind. A minute later the trees up here start rustling.

It's raining now, and he's on the porch watching it wash away the strange patterns of his boot soles in the dirt. Leon's facedown in a growing puddle. It lasts all afternoon and that's fine by Arnett. Flood the whole fucking world.

He's got another jar he found in the shed, or that just came out of nowhere. He's drunk. That's a good thing, too, because the clouds are starting to move. Better get going. So much to do.

Leon's face looks false. Then it looks too real, like it's breathing. But he can tell the life's gone. It's nothing. It's just he's never seen it not breathing, that's all.

He goes through Leon's pockets. No money, just a glass bottle. Opens it and sniffs. "Goddamn. That's my shit. Where'd you get this?" But as soon as he asks he knows the answer. He knows who gave it to him. He takes the shovel's blade, pries Leon's mouth open and pours in the last few drops of the stuff. "How's that taste?" he says.

He can still sense something. Is it what's left of Leon leaving? No, probably ain't nothing.

✕◈✕

Larry stands hiding behind an oak on the western slope of East Ridge, watching Arnett dig. The storm cooled things off and the late summer sun has set clouds afire at the edge of the sky. He'd parked below on the access and was just starting to walk around and check things out when he heard something above him. Then he saw Arnett coming down through the cedars. He ducked behind a tree and hasn't dared move since.

The back of his jacket is soaked from the climb, and the wind chills him. He watches Arnett light a cigarette off the one he just finished, kick the shovel into the ground and bring up dark earth.

The dropping sun spreads like a fan from the earth's edge. It lasts a minute and then it's gone, heating another world.

Far below off to the southwest, the town of Ashland starts glowing down in the basin, small house lights flicker on like the eyes of wolf spiders across a mowed field. His home and the Hickory are safe there in the valley, and that's where he should've stayed. He wants a cigarette but the wind would carry the smoke and give him away. All of a sudden, as if Arnett heard him thinking, he turns downhill and pulls the shovel from the ground.

Larry crouches into the roots and moves farther behind the trunk. Why the hell'd he ever come up here? He should've learned by now he's no good at creeping.

Arnett looks right past him, around him and then announces to no one in particular, "Shovel's a funny thing. Get the whole job done. Multipurpose."

Hands in the wet leaves, Larry holds his balance. His knees hurt. He's out of shape, overweight, not even close to ready for this line of work. Not anymore.

Arnett takes a drag from his cigarette, then kicks the shovel back into the ground. With the sun down, darkness rises from the dirt and leaves and everything beneath. Larry's eyes adjust as Arnett labors over the trench, and after a while there's a pile of roots and dirt and rocks beside it.

Larry's phone is on silent in his pocket. There's not much service up here and you're lucky to even send a text. Sharon's been calling him from their landline. He should've thought to take a picture while it was still light, but he doesn't really know how to do that. He's got Turner's number on speed dial, though. After too many late-night brawls at the Hickory, Turner gave him his personal number and said to call anytime, day or night, if he needed backup. Larry only calls when things get rough. He admires how fast Turner can clear a room, no gun required. Not to say the problems don't escalate once Turner herds them out, but as long as the fighting's outside the barroom, that's all Larry wants. Anyway, the new cops would make this even worse. Ricky and all them—he doesn't trust those guys.

Arnett's almost up to his knees, cursing and digging, when

Larry's phone lights up through the fabric of his windbreaker. He unzips it a few inches and reaches in. Who else? Turner. But the connection will be lost if he opens the phone and answers. Wait to see if he leaves a voicemail. Which he doesn't, goddamn it.

There's no moon yet when Arnett's silhouette, blacker than the night, bends down and rolls what looks like a body into the hole.

The phone lights up again, this time with a text from Turner: *Sharon called said u wernt home where u?*

Arnett's shoveling the mound of dirt into the hole. Larry sinks behind the beech, risks the light of the phone, his hands shaking as he types with his thumbs. *N E ridge off back access come quick.*

Hold tite, Turner replies.

Larry can't think straight. He's trying to stay calm. Keep an eye on Arnett. But the body rolling into the hole, over and over, is all he sees now.

He checks his phone one last time. No service. Great. A fired cop and a tired bartender who used to be a cop. Perfect. Arnett isn't carrying any weapons, as far as Larry can tell, except for the shovel, which is more than he's got.

Arnett's still sitting on a boulder near the mound when headlights finally come stretching through the trees. He drops to the ground and crawls behind the rock. When the car reaches the top it slows to a crawl. Larry watches, holding his breath. Just stop, right here, now.

The car goes past about twenty yards and then brakes. The door opens and the interior light shows Turner toddling out and standing there in the road, holding something in both hands. He's too far away for Larry to see what it is.

"Larry?" Turner yells. "You out here?"

God Jesus. Larry's on his belly, sweating and praying for this shit to be over with. He doesn't want to lose another hand. Or worse. And what's that Turner's bringing up to his shoulder? It's a fucking crossbow.

"Hut-hut-hut! Go long!" Turner yells, releasing an arrow into the treetops. The rushing thuck of it piercing leaves and vines and then whistling off into the sky. The moon has arrived. All goes quiet, and Turner gets back in the car. The red brake lights come on and go off.

The air smells void. Larry tastes copper in his mouth.

Arnett gets to his feet and his face flares with another cigarette. Larry sees the orange dot at the end of it. After a while, Arnett starts whistling to himself and begins moving back uphill toward the inn. He walks into a tree, spins and trips, the cigarette turning and making little line drawings in the dark.

Larry zips his windbreaker up and blows into his hands. It's not cold yet but he's got the chills from sweating. He hears Arnett walking and whistling. He can't tell what tune it is. He'll be goddamned if that guy thinks he can go around acting like this without anybody doing anything about it. But what can Larry do? He's not a cop anymore. And look what happened when he was. He wishes he hadn't seen what he saw.

⁂

Jones's front passenger tire is low on air and slapping against the wet morning road. He's been driving around for a while, stopping here and there to work out chords and words for this new song. Now he's headed west on 15, which will take him back toward the lake, the Hickory, through dead-ass Ashland and on to Natalie's house. The Gibson rests in the passenger seat beside him. "What's wrong?" he says. "You don't have anything to say about any of this?"

He reaches over and flicks the strings above the nut, right below the tuning pegs, bringing a thin, dissonant, high-pitched chime. "That's what I think, too."

Still bourbon brained, he'll grab the case and leave it at that. No extra bullshit. None. They stopped doing that a long time ago. But what if it's not there? Or if she trashed it? That's not out of the question. His father gave him the case and guitar together. He knows better than to leave his shit around her place. Proof of how careless you really are.

He bites down on his tongue, hard, bites until he bleeds, and the flavor of it plus the alcohol from last night makes him heave. He chokes it back, sucks his tongue. The pain keeps his eyes open, alert and on the road.

He drives past a forgotten field of wheat, past random tobacco plants and scrub cedars, piles of trash in plastic bags with drawstrings, derelict farm equipment, collapsing Mail Pouch barns. The road's rough shoulder pulls the low tire into its rut, the van jumps and he pulls back onto the dark pavement rushing toward him.

A straight line going in one direction is all he needs right now. It'll be fine, so calm down. All this worry—it's just his condition talking. The fields are steaming and drying beneath the day's hard sky. He takes the almost empty bottle from between his legs and raises it up. Burns the hell out of his bit tongue. Serves him right.

The last time he saw Natalie was months ago, back when it was cold. They stood waiting at the end of her driveway. For what? A word, a cry—anything to break the paralyzing silence they were trapped in. He doesn't remember what she was wearing, except for that red velvet cowboy hat. When he asked where she got it, she said from over the mountain and that she was planning to make some money with it.

He called her a slut and she smacked him across the face. I

ain't mad at you for saying that, she said. I'm mad at you for not saying it till now.

He drives into a tunnel of river birches, sucking on his tongue. A stretch of swampy land, miles of skeletal branches. A dead coon exploded on the shoulder, its mouth open in a scream. This is the marshland and floodplains of Hickory Lake. Sinkholes you can follow into Kentucky, some that men went missing in forever. Right ahead's the Hickory, then five miles past that is her house. He cruises slowly and takes nips from the bottle, not enough to get drunker, just enough to burn the bite.

Larry's sitting out front on the bench, smoking a cigarette. Shit. Now Jones'll hear all about it. He only needs to get his hat. Grab it, maybe have one beer. He's already half drunk, a beer would be nice.

He gets out of the van, walks up to Larry and stands there with his hands in his pockets. "Just came to get my hat."

"That girl," Larry says without looking up. "She might be the biggest mistake you ever made. You didn't listen to a word she was saying last night."

"Oh, I *heard* her. You actually believed that shit? She just likes getting a rise out of folks, seems to me."

"That right? Well, listen. I drove to Nitro after y'all left and I walked up onto something worse than she even knows about. I saw the guy she was talking about. Arnett. He was digging a grave. Then he rolled something into it."

"What the fuck?"

"I went home and Sharon called the cops. I could've been killed. I run a bar. That's what I do."

"Was it my bass player?"

Larry opens his hands like a book, lays his face in and begins crying. "I'm sorry," he says. "I just ain't slept is all."

Jones watches Larry's thumb rub the thick, fingerless area of his left hand. He never really believed Larry's story about getting shot. He figured he'd just accidentally pulled the trigger on himself, something like that. A careless mistake. But now he's starting to worry. "You didn't do nothing wrong," he says.

"I ain't finished yet."

Jones always wondered if Larry actually came from here, and now that he's crying you can tell he did. When people start crying, their true voice comes out. That was how Jones taught himself to sing.

"Sharon called the cops after I got back," Larry says. "I couldn't even do it. Then I spent the rest of the night talking to these two trooper boys, Ricky and some monkey mouth behind him. They like to bit my head off for calling Turner first."

"Jesus, man. Turner probably wasn't your best choice. Just because y'all were buds in uniform back in the day."

"They came close to arresting my ass. I was like, 'You got a possible murder out there under a foot of dirt on top of that mountain. And you're worried about me?' Look, Jones, you need to stay quiet for a while till this gets sorted out. Things didn't used to be like this, not around here, anyway. You don't need to be playing out right now. At all. Stay low till it blows over."

Jones turns his head sideways, like he's trying to hear something that's too faint to make out. "Things've always been fucked around here. You know that. You need to sleep, man."

"If you're half as smart as you think you are, why'd you go home with Jennifer last night?"

"Jennifer," he says. "My, my."

"You're drunk."

"And you're wrong. We didn't go home. We went to the Lakewood."

"So now where you headed?"

"Over to Natalie's."

"Yep, he's still drunk."

"Get my guitar case, that's all."

"Whatever you do, not a word about Jennifer. Fucking hell, man. You're in some crazy shit. Jennifer's mixed up in it and so are you now. You better stay down."

"Can I play the rest of this week like you said?"

"Didn't you hear me? Somebody's up there dead." He points vaguely toward the mountain. "You can stay at my place and keep quiet about everything. That's what you can do."

"I got to go to Natalie's. Then I'll be back." Instead he might skip around for a day or two, but it's nice to know he's got a spot to go. "If that's all right with you."

"I guess. Don't forget your hat."

"And can I get that box of demos? I'm about broke. Might try to sell a few."

"I paid for those to get made," Larry says. "I'll give them to you. Just promise you won't tell Natalie any of what happened. She'll get to talking. All her friends will too."

Jones pulls a pack from his breast pocket, taps one out and offers one to Larry. "You think we could have a morning pint together, one of them unfiltered whatevers? Just one. My head's hurting bad."

"Well," Larry says, "as long as it's for medicinal purposes."

Behind the bar, he pulls him a cold draft. Sunlight comes in the front window through the jar of pickled eggs on the counter and sends wobbly prisms across the wall. Jones has been in the Hickory this early only once, the time he had to sleep here because Larry hid his keys.

He takes a swallow even before the pint glass touches the bar. It's cold and yellow. Larry tells him to drink it slow, then goes into the kitchen. Jones puts it down and lets it sit there in front of him while he counts to a hundred and twenty.

Pans clatter back there, and by the time the beer's half done Larry comes out with a plate of scrambled eggs, toast and fried bologna. "You're looking pale. Better eat something."

"Yeah, I better." And like a humble bum in prayer, he picks up a fork and leans over the plate.

The van leaves exhaust hanging behind it in the road. Larry sits in a chair in his empty barroom. Jones still hasn't fixed that oil leak. Larry remembers when he was that age, but back then people had more respect. None of this sleeping around business. Well, okay, maybe there was some, but still, folks had more respect for one another. And for themselves, damn it.

He calls Tiff and asks if she can cover the bar the next night or two. "It's going to be a pretty big show this evening," he says. "The Jaguars are playing. I might be around tomorrow to help out."

He closes up but doesn't bother hanging the sign on the locked door. Tiff will be here on time. She's how young people ought to be.

※◇※

*B*ackward, that's how this world is.

Turner got suspended twice for what he calls "necessary unnecessary roughness." When the sheriff, a man going by Ricky, suspended him the second time, Turner swung on him. And Ricky, he told Larry, vanished right in front of him, then reappeared behind him and choked him out. "He's a magical man," Turner said. "I don't mess with magical men no more. I said this to Mr. Ricky, trying to get my job back, I said, 'You are a magical man, Ricky, and I will not mess with you no more.'"

His service Glock was taken from him, along with the badge (not before he xeroxed it)—the only things in life that loaned him any dignity—and though he now operates outside the force, he doesn't carry a gun because the written law is something to be respected. If Turner can't carry firearms, well, so be it, he's got something just as good.

Turner limps in place next to his hubcapless Impala on top of South Hill. The slope where he parked is worn bare from sickly cattle, hoof-patterns in the mud all around him. The wind is strong up here, and he holds down his hair with one hand while the other blocks the sun from his eyes. He squints over toward the Lookout, watching Ricky and a handful of other young uniformed fucksticks string yellow tape around the inn.

They've already been along the ridge. He heard sirens down there near where he'd been last night. Glad he didn't go back looking.

Years ago, when Jack was building this place, Turner was still an officer of the law, but he let the project go. He figured if the construction didn't cause an explosion or collapse into the earth, then the lunatic had earned it. But now he's an officer not by law but by force, the same force he had witnessed and respected in Jack, and he hopes he doesn't have to shoot Arnett, the nephew, with this damn crossbow. But he will if he has to. He once took down a deer from a hundred yards. He aimed high and the arrow just dropped right on top of it. He'd hate to see what it does to a human face. Well, probably just a quick hole and a spot of blood before the guy falls over sideways like in a western.

He reaches through the back window for the crossbow, but it's too wide and gets stuck. He pulls harder and the damn thing goes off. The arrow pierces the seat foam and hits metal. He looks around, opens the door, pulls out the arrow and loads it back into the sliding lock, nicked tip and all.

Clouds chase their shadows over the valley of trees and across the hills and over the ravine and then past the raw clapboard hillbilly palace sitting in the middle of all the mud. From here it looks like a landfill with heaps of stuff and everything smoke gray or clay red. When he passed by on the access last night, that rat bastard was probably running around in the dark. No way was Turner getting out. He'd only stepped out of the car once to let go of an arrow, just to set things straight and get them going on the right track.

The tape's up now and evidently they're done poking around. Arnett's nowhere in sight. Probably watching them from some tree. They're never going to catch him. Look at them, standing around picking their assholes.

Turner brings out his telescope and the Lookout comes into focus. That tin roof, rusted the color of dried blood. The leaning walls and collapsing porch made from unpainted sawmill slabs puzzled together to make a structure that defies all logic and gravity itself. Some stained pink sheets and shirts on the clothes-line in the side yard, advertising what Arnett has been cooking and selling. Probably pretty good stuff.

A couple pigs follow the troopers around and scatter when kicked at. The dogs slink and jog in a wide ring around all the action. They've known nothing but beatings followed by meals of uncooked rice and gunpowder. That's how Turner used to do it, too. Keep them crazy. Great hunters.

He watches the cops gather around Ricky, who's speaking to everyone with his hands in the air everywhere.

"Y'all ain't gonna find this bastard," Turner says, then mouths words to match Ricky's arm movements: "Just, uh, I don't know, go, uh, go get him, go find him, he's got to be somewhere up here, just go get him, hear me?" Ricky goes into the house, and the rest of the men load into patrol jeeps and drive back down the access in a tight line.

Whatever Turner has to do to find Arnett and put him away, it'll happen. This could win him his badge back.

Ricky comes out onto the porch shaking his head, looking around. He gets into the last vehicle left, a tan Bronco with tall antennas, and skids out in a furious tail of gravel dust.

"Ooo-hoo, boys, somebody's frustrated," Turner says.

As the Bronco rolls down the access, he looks up at the widow's walk. There's movement up there. He raises his telescope.

Arnett, looking over the railing.

Son of a mother.

And what the hell's he holding? Turner adjusts the focus. A fiddle case?

Arnett opens a trapdoor and disappears.

Turner waits.

Finally Arnett comes out the front door carrying nothing besides that same case. He starts walking down the access, then cuts off into the woods. Dangerous bastard. Just like his uncle-daddy.

Turner Rides Again, the headlines will say. Picture of Big T standing next to a new cruiser. He scratches the hives breaking out around his groin. Every time his job called for bravery, he got hives like this. At least they don't attack his face. Haven't yet, anyway. So long as they stay in the pants, he can pretend he'll do his duty, no problem. The burn after the scratching feels good. He pisses his underwear just a pinch to hydrate the welts.

So. He'll follow Sapple Lane back down to 231. Cruise that stretch for a while. That's the direction Arnett seemed to be heading. Turner works through his trousers with a clawed hand and continues scanning over to East Ridge. Down in there lies Arnett's mother. It's where Jack used to stash his shine too. He'd bury it in his wife's grave—the one spot nobody ever dared to go. But that ain't the deal now. This is some bona fide bullshit.

Where would Arnett go now that his last refuge is gone? Easy: where he's *not* supposed to go. Misty's. He'll go looking for Bob to ask for money, a place to hide, and that's where Turner will grab him.

※◇※

Arnett wipes cobwebs and dust off the window with his fingers, trying to make out who the hell's parked over there on South Hill. He looks harder but still can't tell. Can't even be sure there is anybody. All he sees in that big pasture is a carlike splotch. It ain't the cops. They already left.

He eats three cans of beans and gets ready for the hike. He can't wait any longer, got to go somewhere. If anybody's watching him, waiting for him, he'll throw them off. He'll walk out the front door like a normal man who just killed out of self-defense, start down the access a little ways and make them think he's headed for 231. Then he'll loop around through the gulch over to the other side of the mountain, jog down the western access to 15 and hitch a ride into Ashland. It's a long walk, but that's what's got to happen. He'll get a room at the Lakewood. They go by the hour there. Buy himself some time to decide what to do.

Burrs are clinging to his shirt and pants by the time he steps out onto 15 with the fiddle case in hand. On the other side of the road are cedar posts holding up miles of wire. In the tall grass beyond, bony heifers stand motionless with their heads bowed. Crazy that they know how to stay alive.

He goes back into the bushes on the westbound shoulder and through the leaves he can see every car coming down off the mountain. Heat dances in the distance. No cars at all.

The cows drift closer, heads lifted and mouths chewing sideways circles in stupid curiosity. His stomach twists in pain. A truck roars toward him but it's some kind of business rig. Can't do that.

Finally a sedan comes crawling through the heat waves like a mirage. He steps onto the shoulder holding his thumb out.

He pulls on the handle but it's locked. When the electric window whines open a crack, he feels air-conditioning and smells chewing gum. "Where you going?" the man behind the wheel asks. "Do you smoke?"

"Just into Ashland," Arnett says.

"Do you believe in aliens?"

Arnett ignores that. "Yeah," he says. "I smoke."

"I can't take you, then. You're the test subject of a long-term extraterrestrial experiment. That's why they have you smoking. I'm at risk already. They're probably tapping this conversation right now."

"Then why'd you stop?"

"Glory desert."

Arnett blinks.

"I saw you were a musician." He puts a piece of gum into his mouth.

Arnett lifts the case up to the window and opens it, revealing a Smith & Wesson revolver with a barrel the length of an indecent man's organ. "You ever been shot in the face before?"

The car rips onto the road and tears off over the crest. Arnett goes back to hide and wait. He lets a couple trucks pass, then sees another sedan.

A wife and husband up front, three blond baby boys in back. Behind the wheel, the man sips bottled water and tells his kids to make some room. They stare at Arnett like the stranger he is before sliding over against the door. He gets in and puts the case in his lap, and the boy sitting next to him touches it. "You don't want that," Arnett says.

"And are you a musician?" the wife says, smiling through the puffed layer of skin covering her face.

"These triplets?" Arnett says.

"Sure are," the man says. "You play music?"

"Sure are," Arnett says.

The man pulls back onto the highway and Arnett watches the power lines rising and falling in rhythm. Kudzu creeps up from the woods down to the roadside and climbs the tall wooden electric poles. Eventually the lines fly away down another road. The closest boy puts a toy up on Arnett's leg and he brushes it off. The boy starts crying and the mother tells him not to bother their guest, but the kid gets louder and howling red. Arnett doesn't pick up the toy car. The mother reaches over the seat and puts it back in her son's lap. "He's your neighbor, Matthew," she says. The boy starts calming down. "And how are you supposed to treat your neighbors?"

"Like us," he recites.

When they reach Ashland, the husband points toward the old bait shop ahead. "How's this?" he says.

"Just a little farther up. To the Lakewood."

"Oh, let's buy him a room," the wife says to the man.

The wife hands Arnett some money and he gets out of the car. It looks like she's trying to remember a question. The trees and buildings are all brown from the mill. His hair blows upward in the wind like it's about to fly off his scalp. Before shutting the door, he leans back inside, takes the boy's little red car and says, "I ain't your neighbor."

At the Lakewood Arnett pays for eight hours in a hole with a peeling carpet and a small window that looks out on the U-Haul trucks across the street. The key ring they gave him has a rubber fish dangling from it. He puts the fiddle case down on the bed. The U-haul sign has a flashing arrow with lightbulbs underneath the lettering, *We Help You Leave.* He shuts the blinds, kicks his boots off and collapses on the bed next to the case.

When he wakes up, the digital clock says he has three hours left.

He flips TV channels to forget what he saw in his sleep. A woman trying to sell him jewelry. Somebody drowning. A preacher laying bodies out across a stage with the touch of his palm. Arnett sits up on the edge of the mattress, listening to the tele-sermon and looking at his palms. "If only."

He lies back down, feet still hanging off the end, the TV going on about how evil is real. When he wakes up again he hears a voice outside. It's too good to have even been prayed for. "Yes, please," he says.

He gets up, sticks a finger into the blinds and there she stands in the glowing light of a Coke machine, checking the options and singing. Jennifer, you little fucking sweetheart. Should've known she'd be hiding out here. Just like him.

When he opens the door, the damp thickness of evening air rolls into the room. No light besides the Coke machine and a flickering parking lamp at the other end of the lot. Behind her, he clears his throat and says, "Jenny Penny? You mind? I'm trying to sleep. Come here."

She doesn't even try to run. Can't.

"I," she breathes, like recovering from a punch in the gut.

It looks like she might cry, something he's never seen her do. "What's wrong?"

"I," she says.

"Yeah, you." He takes her wrist and leads her into his room. She drags her feet, doesn't resist, doesn't say no. She never did.

———

He sits her down on the bed and tells her not to move or speak. He stays still and silent too, studying her face while some preacher on the TV says, "Did you know you could be just one minute from hell?" Arnett shakes his head as the voice continues. "I was one time a minute away from hell and did not realize it, my Lord, my mighty Christ, He took me in as the shepherd will the lamb, and He showed me it began in the darkest hour like it always does, that I'd been around family and friends my whole life and still found myself so alone, and you could be too, just one short minute from hell."

"Quit this," she says.

Instead Arnett improvises his own sermon, wiping tears from his eyes. "The day He come to me, it was the most mysterious thing. Almost out of nowhere. Like back from the grave. Jesus come from a place you never been. Never seen before. Someplace you don't come back from. Not usually. That's what makes him Him. Your Jesus, He come back from the dead. For you. He rose from that grave with a sword."

She bolts for the door, her head rushing with noise, but Arnett kicks in the back of her knee and she falls down. He sits on her and slaps his hand over her mouth and won't let her scream.

"Keep that shit in your throat," he says. "You got no idea of the physical pain that goes along with coming back to life after dying." A tear falls from his eye and lands on her face. She's kicking and trying to get out from under him but he's so heavy and eventually she gets tired and can hardly breathe. He takes her by the hand, pulls her up and turns the TV off. She sits back down on the worn carpet floor, her hair in her face. "Pretty like always," he says, opening a fiddle case. "If you keep quiet I'll play you the 'Tennessee Waltz.'"

"I don't need you playing nothing for me," she says. "I want you to let me out of this room before I scream and somebody gets in here."

"Like who?"

"Leon knows where I am."

"Lie number ten thousand and fucking one."

"He'll be here soon."

"I saw him last night. He really wasn't looking so hot. Said he wouldn't be able to make it."

"What'd you do to him?"

"What he did to *me*. What *you* did to me."

"I don't know what you're talking about," she says.

"You're a crazy fucking lying bitch, too."

"I *will* scream."

"It won't be loud as this." He reaches into the case and shows her what it carries. "I want us back together. We were made to be together. We can make it work, baby. We *going* to make it work." He's not really talking to her but to the gun, considering it with a country deference and running his fingers over the tarnished silver plate on the grip engraved with a J. "Don't try leaving," he says.

She doesn't say anything back.

"Scream all you want," he says. "Want to scream, go right ahead. It's nothing these walls ain't heard before. A good old loud fuck. Hey, that gives me an idea."

She covers her face and peeks through her fingers as he goes back to the fiddle case and takes out a little jar of cloudy corn whiskey. He looks through it right at her and drops it into her lap. "Drinky," he says.

She looks up, stares into him. "I ain't drinking this shit."

He rams the nose of the pistol into the bed pillow. "We're going to," he says. "I'll go first." He puts the gun in his belt and snatches the jar from her lap. She cringes at the skirling sound of the lid being twisted off. He takes a drink, then hands it to her.

Jennifer figures she might actually just get shot tonight. Here is the man she helped poison. He's lost his mind. But doesn't she deserve it? He has every right in the world. No, hell no. It's not about what *she* deserves. It's about what he'll actually *do*. She takes a sip.

"That's enough," he says. "Give it here."

He takes most of what splo's left in one swallow, then starts ranting about reasonable reasons they should work through their differences. One last swig and he's stumbling, like somebody turned out the light. "Tell you what." He leans to one side and pulls the pistol from his belt. "I ain't gonna shoot you."

"Please don't."

"*If*," he says.

"If?"

"If you tell me who else you been hunching."

"I ain't been."

Arnett shuts his eyes, tests the air with his nose.

I'm about to get shot, she thinks. He can smell the lie.

"You stink like cock," he says. "And look at your face. Who touched you?"

It tastes like her lips are bleeding again. Knowing she's too far gone to take anything back, she doesn't speak or move.

"Hey," he says. "Guess what. I got a present for you."

She keeps focused on the black hole at the end of the barrel while he reaches into his pocket with his free hand. He holds out a tiny red racing car in front of her face.

"Where'd you get that?" She can't help but laugh. "You steal it from a little kid or something?"

XOX

When Jones rolls into Natalie's duplex lot, he's feeling brave. He noses the van into the space next to her Chrysler, then thinks better of it, pulls out, turns around and backs it in facing out.

At the top of the stoop, he sees the front door's wide open behind the screen and letting the heat of the day into the house. But this isn't his life anymore. Without knocking he pulls the screen door and walks inside.

The coffee table in front of the entertainment center is crowded with empties that spill over onto the carpet in puddles and shards. An open handle of something cheap lies sideways on the couch. Ashtrays overflowing. It smells like every song he's ever sung.

But there's a new addition, right under the coffee table: a crusted pipe, ziplocked in with some rocks and the rest of the mix.

The La-Z-Boy is reclined flat with a comforter over it and a man's hairy foot poking out. Jones clears his throat at whoever it is. No response, so he pulls the blanket back to reveal a familiar face swollen from sleep and whatever else. Raw stubble around the open mouth and spreading up the cheekbones.

"Eads," he says, but Eads doesn't move. Jones holds a finger under his nose like a mustache to check his breathing. "Wake up, you fuckrag."

When he's turning away, the blanket gets thrown open and it's Terri, lying right behind Eads, snuggled up cute as a critter. "Hey, bubby," she says.

"What the hell's going on in here?" Jones says.

Terri starts laughing. "Hey, we're finished," she says, gets up, fetches the bottle of Montezuma from the couch and crawls back under the blanket. "We's just trying to stay cool is all," she says. "Shoot, looks like it's only enough for one." She holds it up to the blue TV light and then takes a kiss from it. "Mmn-mmn, good morning, daddy." She slides the rest of the way under the covers.

"You seen Natalie?" Jones says.

"We tried getting her in on this. But she won't leave her room."

"I had nothing to do with it, Jones," Eads says.

"Bull," Terri says. "It was your idea."

"Natalie," Eads says. "Goddamn Natalie. Where she at? Where that bitch go? And why's it so fucking hot in here?"

"Y'all left the door open, geniuses."

"Nuh-uh," Terri says. "Door's broke. It just don't close. Opening ain't its problem."

"What in the hell's wrong with y'all?"

The question seems to focus Eads. "The shit they got coming off that mountain, baby, it's like, it's . . ." He starts pushing his eyeballs around with his pointer fingers. "There's more than a human can handle. But one guy runs it all around, from here down to Kingsport. We became friends. Motherfucker's a hero. I'll give you his number, if you want. We're friends. He calls me. And since me and you's friends, I'll give you his number. You can call him up. Now where's Natalie?"

"You crazy!" Terri slaps her hand over Eads's mouth.

"Must've been a fun night," Jones says. "I'll try her room."

At the end of the hallway he finds the door locked and hears the noise of a window unit rattling inside. He bangs on the door and tries the knob. "Natalie? It's me, your evil ex-husband. I'm here for my guitar case."

He stands there with his ear to the door, nothing, then goes to the kitchen to find a drink and think about whether he shouldn't just break into her room. He feels like kicking something down.

He checks in the cupboard, but that's where *he* used to keep it. Under her rules of operation it's below the sink, where a bottle of bourbon is next to a can of Drano. While he's pouring whiskey into a can of flat Coke he found, an icy hand touches the back of his neck. Natalie. Her eyes raccooned in mascara. Lipstick smeared. Hair tangled into a nest atop her little head.

"Look," Jones says, holding up both hands, "all I want—"

"Your case is fine. Have a good time being gone?"

She's still toasted, Jones can smell it.

Under the blanket, Eads whispers to Terri, "That's Natalie. Get her under here."

"Don't pay them no mind," Natalie says to Jones. "They just been to the Big Rock Candy Mountain."

"If I'm interrupting something I can come back later."

She tightens her hair. "Come back in the kitchen."

"Just give me my case," he says.

"We miss you," she says, holding her breasts and moving them up and down. Jones follows her. She opens the fridge and takes out a tin can emptied of tomatoes and now full of red wine. The top's still hanging on where the can opener didn't catch. "Come back to my room," she says.

"Look, I thought we settled this. I just need—"

"I know what you fucking need. So come back and get it."

Jones pushes past her to the bedroom. His case better be in there.

She stays right on his heels down the hall. Her closet door's off its hinges and leaning against the window. No light ever gets in here. Jones sees the guitar case in the closet.

Natalie slams the door shut behind them. "Here I am," she says.

He checks all five latches to make sure the case doesn't fly open, then takes it up by the leather handle. It molds to his hand. But Natalie's standing right behind him with the can of wine to her mouth. When she stops for a breath, Jones pushes her aside and opens the door.

"Just like trash," she says. "That's how you're throwing me away. Like trash."

He makes it down the hallway with her screaming on his heels, picks up the Coke can from the coffee table where he left it and throws it back. He turns and sees her standing in the dark. He feels the whiskey coming on. "Natalie," he says. "Don't make it worse."

She leans against the wall, unbuttons the top of her pants and yanks down her zipper. "I'm just trying to make it better."

Knowing he's got a song to write helps him look at her and say, "No."

"What's her name?" Natalie says.

"This is stupid."

"Not as stupid as what I'm going to do if you don't tell me." She points at the blanket.

"Have fun, then," Jones says.

She jumps at him, and before he can move she tosses the rest of her wine in his face.

Eads starts laughing. "Come on over, y'all. Plenty of room."

Jones wipes the wine from his eyes.

"Tell me what her name is," she says.

He shouldn't say it. Everybody's listening. Don't do it.

※◇※

Arnett rears back to hit her with the pistol. She blocks her face, but nothing happens.

"God, fuck it," he says. "You know I only do this because I love you. Everything I do, it's because I love you."

"If you did, we wouldn't be here like this. You got me trapped in a motel room, and all you do is pretend you're gonna hit me? Do it or don't. Just quit pretending."

"There ain't no going back." He paces in front of her. "What's done is done."

"It *ain't* done," she says. "Please."

"Say some more words and I'll put a bullet through your tongue. Say fucking words! You hear me now?"

"What am I supposed to do?" she says. "All you ever did was torture me."

"Bull fucking horse shit."

The gun's still on her but he seems to be listening now. "Put it down," she says.

"You asked for every single thing I ever did to you."

"Look at us," she says. "You with a gun. How's this making things better?"

"Last night," he says. "Let's start there and go backwards."

"I was right here."

"With who?"

"None of your business," she says. "Besides, nobody."

"Oh, it's definitely my business." Arnett steps at her with the pillow and she pushes herself up, her knees hurting from sitting folded and all her nerves going, like she's about to shit herself. She grabs for the pillow, expecting a bullet, but he pulls it away. She lunges at him and a flashing explosion stops them both. The smell of burnt hair fills the room, a high-pitched ringing in her ears. Pieces from the wall behind her crumble onto the floor.

"I told you hush," he says.

The shot glanced her shoulder, knocked her back a few feet. She puts her hand over the pain moving and growing like a burning web. "You shot me?" she says.

"No I didn't."

She keeps her hand over the pumping blood. "God," she says. "My God."

"Always disagreeing with me. I give you a place to live, and all you give me is what?"

"I gotta sit down."

"Do that."

She folds into the chair over in the corner and it feels like her feet aren't there. This, she understands, is shock.

"Now." Arnett puts the gun back in the fiddle case and locks it shut. "Let me go get you some water. I never shot a girl before."

Instead, he takes a notepad from his pocket, picks up the phone and starts trying numbers, crashing the receiver back into the cradle every time nobody answers, until somebody finally does.

"Eads," he says. "Arnett calling. Very serious question. You hear me? What? Wait." He holds the receiver out from his face. "Shit-ass phone," he says, and goes over to the keypad until he finds a button and hits it.

A man's voice talks through the static of the speakerphone: "Questions are serious because they're asking something."

"Don't fuck with me, Eads," Arnett says.

"Don't fuck with *me*, man! I paid your ass! These questions, they always ask people for, like, fucking answers."

"You won't have to pay me for nothing, Eads, if you'd just shut up for a second. Zero payments."

"Zero? Without any numbers in front?"

"None."

"Listening."

"Where's your car at? I need to borrow it. Can you bring it to me?"

"Is that really you, Arnett? Terri, it's him on the phone. Yeah! Bring us more Robot, Arnett!"

"It's me. Come on, man. Wake up. I need your car."

"Me and Terri's locked, baby."

"Your car," Arnett says. "Tell me where it's at. I'll bring you both some Robot, for free, if you just tell me where your fucking car's at."

"I have a car. Yes. Where you?"

"With Jennifer. Wake up and think. Tell me where your car is."

"Jennifer. Woozy! Why didn't you say so? I was at Natalie's this morning, when this dude, Jones—you know him?"

"Fuck." Jennifer tries to sit up but the walls are warped and the floor's slanted and the chair she's in keeps tumbling backwards.

"That sorry-ass country singer from Misty's," Arnett says. "Yeah."

"He came by fighting with Natalie. You should've heard them. She was yelling and throwing shit at him and then he starts telling her how he slept with some girl, some slut named Jennifer. This very morning. I didn't know if it was your Jennifer or not. But the name jumped out at Terri, and she told me I better tell you. Was it your Jennifer?"

"That's a good question," Arnett says, looking straight at her. "Sounds to me like some cut-rate hunch."

She puts her hands on the arms of the chair and warm blood pumps from her shoulder. Focus, she tells herself. Keep it together until this is over. It's almost over.

"Where's the Robot?" Eads says. "Come on, let's go. How the hell you gonna get it to us without a car?"

Arnett rips the phone cord from the wall.

Jennifer sees him go into the bathroom and then he comes out holding a plastic cup. He sets it on the table beside her. "Drink you some water," he says, but she can barely understand. Everything's moving so fast now and he's talking about getting out of here before somebody comes knocking. "Where's the keys to your truck?" he says, and begins going through her purse. "They in your room?" Arnett dumps the purse onto the bed. Gum wrappers, ChapStick, receipts, a multi-tool, a wallet. He stuffs bills from the wallet into his pocket. There's her license. He'll leave that so the ambulance can identify her. He unzips an inside pocket in the purse, reaches in and feels the keys.

"Don't do me like this," she says.

He tosses the keys in the air and snatches them. "Who'd you hook up with last night? Why's your face all busted? You been hooking? Who with? Tell me that."

She tries to stand but can't. "That's my business," she says. "And besides, I been right here the whole time."

"With Jones."

"Who's Jones?"

"Maybe you didn't get his name before he left this morning," Arnett says. "Jones—Natalie's Jones?"

"I didn't do shit."

"Your friendly friend you fucking fucked this morning," Arnett says. "He plays at Misty's. Shitty-ass country. Don't worry if your mind's not working. That's what losing blood does to you. I'll find him for you."

She picks up the cup of water, drinks and rests it between her legs. "I didn't."

"You did. And I'm taking your truck."

She winces, grips her arm. "I'm sorry."

"Too late for that." He brings her more water.

The wallpaper in here is playing tricks in her eyes. It's close and far away. Moving and still. Coming in and going out.

"Drink your water."

"Arnett," she says. "You go get somebody. I need help."

He stands in the door looking back. A broken glow around his body. Bugs flying in around him. "I'm definitely going to go get somebody. Now drink your water."

※◇※

Turner busts into Durty Misty's holding a xerox of his old badge in one hand and the loaded crossbow in the other, swinging it around and yelling for everybody to clear the fuck out, move-move-move, code red, code red, everybody out, we got a code red.

When he sees it's Turner, a single scream leaves Old Bob's mouth and then he's out the door and in his car and gone.

The drunks remain calm, picking up their lighters and cigarettes. Not really many of them. They almost seem thankful somebody's forcing them to leave.

It doesn't take long to empty Misty's out. Never did.

Turner came here to break up a fight once. Bob was the one that called him. The men had been brawling for half an hour, everybody watching and shouting with every swing. Grown men hitting each other in the face for that long. Some serious damage. Turner watched them going at it and wouldn't let anybody leave the barroom until they finished. He held his gun on them, the spotlight in the cruiser's dash shining on them through the window. He reminded the peckernecks that somebody better fall and not get up, or else.

Eventually one of them did, a guy named Kenny. Turner bought a beer for the winner, somebody from Ohio called Lewis the Linebacker. Turner drove Kenny home. He looked bad but was breathing fine and the wife took him in without a word. Just another Friday night.

But later when Lewis was drinking his victory beer he fell flat on his face on the table. His friends shook him, tried waking him up. But he wasn't asleep. He was dead. He had died, and Kenny was just fine.

Now wasn't that some shit. When the winner ain't the winner. Turner sits at the empty bar alone. Arnett, man. You best show up.

※◇※

There's a bum camp in a run-down state park off 15 East. Jones used to come here to get ideas for songs. He's here now just for the company of men who have it worse than he does. That and he needs a nap.

The sign on the front gate reads *Closed for the Winter,* over which someone has spray-painted *Forever.* He pulls around the gate, drives over the knocked-down chain-link fencing and parks in a derelict campsite in the shade of tall pines. There's a warped picnic table and a grill cemented into the ground. He puts the windows halfway up for mosquitoes and shuts off the engine. The deep quiet of the forest, the endless rustling and bending and prickling of the pines—this is what being out among the stars would sound like. He opens the guitar case, cracks a can of Busch. The campsite where the guys stay is farther back toward the railroad tracks. El Rancho Relaxo, they call it. He'll go find them in a little bit. He begins fingerpicking— and the rest of the words to the song he's been thinking about nearly pour out of his mouth. He works on them for a while, switching verses around and trying to come up with a chorus that feels natural but unlocks the song with some surprise. He doesn't want to sound clever. He hates clever songs. That's not him. Never was. A guitar in his lap and a few brews left on the floor—hard to believe you could ever want anything more than a summer day alone in a van with a guitar. And no girls allowed.

He drinks another beer, eats a piece of fried chicken he bought at a gas station and falls asleep on the floor under the backseat on top of his stinking sleeping bag and his boots for a pillow. He wakes up in the afternoon to hear the call of a barred owl: *Who books for you? Who books for you?* He's never heard one in daylight before. But it's true, who books for him? Maybe he does need an agent.

The van's side is catching sun and it's getting hot in here. He reaches for the ignition and rolls down the electric windows, letting out his fumes. It takes a while for the forest air to come in. He's in no rush. He rests his head back and closes his eyes. This morning's hangover is finally gone, thank holiness. When was the last morning he didn't wake up with one? Maybe once in the last five years. Maybe not. With his eyes closed, his mind feels open. Ready to be filled. Nothing but time here.

He sits up again, looks out the window and sees a ragged man in a disaster of a jumpsuit not twenty yards away, pumping water from a rusted spigot. Trying to, at least. He gets out of the sleeping bag, pulls on his boots and crawls from the van. At first he doesn't notice how old the man is. But walking over, he sees white hairs curling out from beneath his cap, around his black forehead and down his face.

"You need any help there?" Jones says.

The man holds his hands in front of his face, inspecting them like they were two pieces of a tool that should never have come apart. Then he considers the pump handle. "Well sure," he says.

Jones pumps it a few times and cold groundwater flows out.

"You don't remember me," the guy says.

Jones turns back to him. The long white beard, yellow around the mouth from nicotine. Brown pupils painted onto yellow eyeballs. The missing teeth. The big smile. "Cory," Jones says.

"I thought you about didn't recognize me."

"I didn't."

"Now you do, though, now you do." He slips a galvanized pail under the spigot and Jones watches the water rush and swirl into it. All that shapeless water taking form. Jones keeps pumping until it's filled.

"Thank you, boy."

"I ain't your boy," Jones says.

"Then your mama's a liar." He puts up his dukes while Jones air-boxes at him. "It's good to see you. You was on the road."

"I was. I'm back. I'm hitting solo. Too much stress trying to keep musicians in line."

"You been to Nashville?"

"You always ask me that. Yeah, we were there. Just weren't prepared enough to be playing in front of those folks. Fuck that shit anyhow."

"Yessir, I was there. That was ten, naw, shoot, fifteen years ago. When you go back, you tell that man Randy I said hi. I wrote a song while I was there. Sang it to some talent finder and soon before I knew it that song was on the radio without me even knowing. Got to be careful who you show your music to. But Randy's all right."

"You've told me that story before," Jones says.

"And ain't a bit changed. Because it's true."

"I'll be careful." Jones can tell by how Cory's rambling that he's been at the campsite for a long time. Close to the rail line here, and thirty minutes down the highway there's the junk stores around I-81. That must be where he goes for his amenities.

Cory catches a few drops from the spigot, lifts his cap and runs his wet hand through his hair. "You want some dinner?"

"What time is it?"

"Dinner time. Though you look about half asleep. You want some coffee?"

"I wouldn't turn it down."

"I'll show you what we got going on around here. Bring that bucket."

Jones jogs back to the van for his guitar, then grabs the water and follows. They come through a thicket into a clearing with tarps and tents. An old camper covered with emerald moss sits there flat-tired. Smoke rises from coals in the middle of the camp, where a man with cheeks full of scars sits at the fire in layers of sweatpants and hoodies under a yellow poncho, his palms hovering toward the flames. He looks like he's been in this same spot, in the same clothes, in the same position, since last winter. It's possible.

"That's Eddie," Cory says. "He always cold. Welcome home, Jones."

Jones sets down the water pail and the guitar case and takes a seat on a cinderblock across from Eddie, who's still warming his hands back and forth as if it's a long ritual that requires relentless concentration.

"How you?" Jones says.

Eddie looks up and stares past him with cloudy gray eyes.

Jones can see he's blind.

Cory walks up to the fire with an iron skillet, the handle broken off, and some cans of Vienna sausages. He lays the skillet on glowing branches that crumble under the weight. Cory rips the tops off the cans and dumps in the small pallid cylinders of meat.

"You ain't got no tobacco on you, do you?" Cory says.

Jones takes a pack of Camels from his shirt pocket, hands him one and takes out another for Eddie.

"Eddie here suffers from blindness of the physical eyes," Cory says. "But I swear he'll surprise you with what-all he sees. Stuff I don't even recognize."

"Y'all are doing all right out here," Jones says.

"I'd sooner be here than that shelter," Cory says.

"I know that's right," Eddie says.

"People like that man coming around. What's his name?"

"Arnett," Eddie says.

"Arnett," Cory says. "Coming around and paying folks like us off to do things. His things."

Eddie shakes his head. "I tell you," he says. "I stick to my own things. I don't need no other folks' things."

"Ar-fucking-nett," Jones says. "His father shot my best friend. Bad blood in that pack. What things does Arnett pay y'all to do?"

Eddie makes the motions of smoking from a pipe and then jerking off. "Y'all white folks can keep it," he says.

After the meal, Cory brings out a pint of gin and he and Eddie pass it back and forth. They offer it to Jones, who holds up a hand. "I still got some driving left," he says.

"You a good boy," Cory says. "I always knew that. Take you some of that coffee there."

Jones asks if he can play them a song he's been working on. Not sure what he's thinking about calling it. After the first verse and chorus, he makes up words for a second verse; he's forgotten some of what he came up with before he fell asleep, and he stops in the middle. "I'm still fooling with it," he says.

"Sing that first part again," Eddie says. "Faster like."

"And really beat that guitar," Cory says. "Give it hell."

Jones begins, "If I had my way, I'd leave here tomorrow, hitch up a ride and ride on down to Mexico. But there's just one thing I gotta do . . ."

"Wait, wait, wait now," Eddie says. "Hell yeah. That even the same song?"

"It is," Cory says. "It's the same words. But he ain't afraid of them strings no more. Now the song's missing just the one thing. What about the pussy? Give me that here."

Jones hands over the guitar. Cory makes a C chord correctly but a fret too high. Still, he strums. "I wrote this one I'm gonna sing," he says. "'I got friends in low places . . .'"

"No chance they get any lower than this," Jones says. "Here, give it back."

"So you're leaving town, or want to," Eddie says. "And you got one thing you gotta do. What is it? It better be damn good. 'Cause we all got shit we gotta to do. But do we do it?"

"Hell naw!" Cory says.

"You don't know that," Eddie says. "Give the boy back his guitar and let's see."

Jones takes a pick out of his pocket. Don't rush it, just drive it. "There's just one thing I gotta do," he sings, "and I don't want murder on my soul." He flatpicks the melody and rises into the chorus, now remembering the words and their feel: "I don't want murder on my soul, dear mother, I don't want murder on my soul. Just one thing I gotta do—and I don't want murder on my soul."

"That's it, that's right," Cory says. "Sing it."

Strumming and humming, Jones looks up, trying to remember. "Can't think how the rest goes."

"It's *done*," Eddie says. "That thing's *done*. Done and done. Cory, next song."

Cory starts into "Ninety-Nine Bottles of Beer on the Wall," which he says he also wrote, and Eddie begins belting it out with him. Cory looks at Jones. "You know we ain't gonna stop till you give us money for some."

❌◇❌

Larry knocks and Sharon cracks open the door, the chain pulling taut as she peers out.

"It's okay," he says. "It's just me."

"I can see that." She unlatches the chain.

He drags from his cigarette, bends and stubs it in the bucket of sand. He steps past her, leaving the door for her to shut.

"Don't bring all that inside with you," she says, fanning out the smoke.

"It's hot in here," he says.

He holds the doorframe to the kitchen for balance while stepping on the heel of his shoe to get it off. "I'm not working tonight," he says. "Probably not tomorrow."

"Don't you have the Jaguars booked tonight? That's the show you were counting on this month. We can't dip into any more savings."

"Tiff's got it covered." He goes into the kitchen.

"Like hell she does."

"She's a good girl, Sharon."

"When you're around."

"You don't know."

"I've heard stories."

"We're not starting this right now."

He picks the phone off the counter and dials Turner's number. It rings a while. Of course. It's Turner. The light angles in through the window and slips across the table. Larry hasn't been in the house at this hour of the day in a long time. Sharon's standing in the doorway watching him.

He covers the receiver with his hand. "Just a minute, Share. I'm just . . ."

Finally Turner answers. "Yeah, what?"

When Larry holds up his index finger, she throws her hands in the air and goes back into the living room.

"Who's calling Turner at this hour?" Turner says. "Who?" He sounds beer drunk.

"It's Larry. I got to tell you something."

"That's better. Report findings."

"Listen, Turner. This is about Arnett."

"Where's he at?"

"I don't know. But I got to tell you. I called the cops."

"I saw them. I'll forgive you this time. Guess who else I saw. Him. This morning at the Lookout. Ricky and them missed him entirely."

"Why didn't you take him?"

"I didn't say I was *there*. I was over on South Mountain, surveilling the place. Anyways, I know where he's going."

"So why you asking if I know where he's at?"

"Old trooper-trust exercise. Remember? Don't worry. You passed."

"How you plan on finding him?"

"I been doing my research. He can't stay on that mountain forever. Where's the one place in the county he still has a friend?"

"You tell *me*," Larry says.

"Misty's," Turner says. "He gonna come looking for little old Bobby."

"But how in the hell would he rationalize going into Bordon? You need to call the real cops about what you saw."

"They already had their chance," Turner says. "This here's mine. Listen, Larry, you let me know if you want to get in on this. We could ride again, buddy."

"What's that supposed to mean?"

"I'm just saying. I know you itching for some action."

"I've had enough of it. I like who I am."

"This could be your chance to get back in the business. A big catch."

"Aw, come on. I ain't about to get mixed up in this shit."

"Dollars."

"You need to leave this to the cops. I hate to say it—I shouldn't have even called you."

"I *am* the cops," Turner says. "And now everybody's gonna fess up to that and pay me for the safety I provide."

"Are you drinking?"

"I'm sitting here in Misty's right now. Staked out."

"Shit," Larry says. "If I don't hear you've straightened things by midnight, I'm calling Ricky myself and telling him everything you just told me."

"You don't trust Ricky any more than I do. They should've been there for you when you were in court with Jack. They could've pressed your warrant, validated the CPS call and convicted that monster. Instead they made you go it alone."

"I don't need any reminders. It's done now and I'm living a good life."

"I know exactly what's going on. And let me say this. What Arnett's done is huge. Everything all over again. I know you know." He pauses, and Larry hears him take a swallow. "And it's right in line with what's been going on over there for ten years on that mountain."

"All I'm saying . . ."

"If you don't wanna join my force," Turner says, "stay out of it from here on."

"I absolutely do not. You by yourself there?"

"I did some sweeping earlier."

Larry looks up and sees Sharon stepping into the kitchen. "Well, don't make a mess of it," he says. "If he shows up, that's when you call the cops."

The phone cuts off. Sharon leaves the room and Larry just sits there. He hears her go out the front door. She stays gone for a while. Then she comes back, holding out her cell phone. "I just called the police, Larry, and told them to go check on Turner. He's at Misty's, right? I don't mean to be getting in your business. But I do not trust that man. I want to make sure you're safe. That's the first thing I care about. I hope you're not mad."

Larry stares at nothing. "No, no," he says. "That's the right thing to do."

"Do you believe that?"

"No."

"Do you hate me for calling them?"

"No."

She runs her fingers through his hair, and then holds his face in her hands. "You're exhausted. Let's go lie down."

"I don't know how to handle this stuff," he says.

"I know it," she says. "Why should you?"

She gets some candles going, pours him a glass of wine, puts a chicken in to roast and boils some potatoes. She makes sure he eats a lot.

Now she waits for all that food and the wine and TV to do what they're supposed to do to a man. Put him to sleep. Set his mind at rest. Plus the sound of rain beginning to patter on the roof. They're lounging together on the couch. She points the remote at the TV and turns it off so it's just the raindrops and each other.

Larry's having the hardest time he's ever had. She can feel him worrying. And she knows he's worried for Jones Young, who's like a son to him. Those two have helped each other through so much, and now Larry doesn't know how to go about helping him. Just as she doesn't know how to go about helping Larry.

Palpable's the word that keeps coming to her. *Palpable*. She learned that one when she took a class at the community college. She's always liked words, and though she doesn't know too many, *palpable*'s like when somebody doesn't respect you and won't say so but you know it. You can feel it. That's palpable. Her first husband sure was. Or when somebody loves you so much they don't even need to say it. That's palpable too. Guess what Larry is?

His feet are on the armrest right next to her head. She finds one with her free hand, squeezes it, then rolls off the couch, careful not to spill the open bottle of red onto the carpet.

"Cork that thing, will you," Larry says without looking.

"Say what?"

"Please," he says.

She looks at him lying there. Why won't he quit staring at

the ceiling? Ever since that phone call to Turner, she's been waiting for him to fall asleep so she can check up on things and see if they found him. "You sure you don't want any more wine?" she says.

"Ask me one more time and I just might take some so you'll quit asking."

"Well, then." She pours him another glass. "Want another, want another, want another?"

"Thank you." He sits up and throws it back.

"You'll cause a leak up there if you keep staring."

She takes the bottle into the kitchen and looks at the answering machine for messages, even though she knows nobody's called.

She washes their dishes, the pot she boiled the potatoes in. She dries everything off with a hand towel, puts everything away and then opens the oven. There's the rest of that chicken, mostly just bones and some scalded skin around the legs. She should clean that up before it dries out and sticks to the baking sheet, but she doesn't feel like dealing with it right now. She'll start soup out of it tomorrow morning, leave it be for tonight. She cooked a meal for a man she loves. Nothing beats that.

In the living room, Larry's pulled the quilt off the back of the couch and tossed it over his knees, his head turned to the side, his eyes closed. She says his name and he furrows his brow. She watches him for a while, kneels down beside him, says his name again. He's out.

She goes back to the kitchen, picks up the phone and puts in a request for an officer to check on the Hickory after they check on Misty's. The operator asks her to hold. She can feel something's up. It's palpable.

※◇※

Driving Jennifer's truck back to the Lookout, Arnett stops at the only station on this side of 15, fills the tank and splits before paying. He looks in the side mirror to see a woman trotting out to the pumps, cell phone to her head.

Fuck the speed limit. Fuck the limit of speed. He found a little bit in Jennifer's glove compartment in a baggie and it was already crushed. Probably his at one point, his now for sure. Pain erupts in his belly and causes him to swerve. Stay on the road. He never thought being a liquorholic would work to his favor, but he ain't dead yet. It's like he's been training his gut for this very occasion.

The tires over wet asphalt sound like a long sheet of paper getting torn and torn and torn. The Buzzard Hollow sign flashes on the right. That road rolls up and down along East Ridge for hours into Kentucky, then flattens out once you hit Tennessee. A wild ride with lots of little pull-offs onto unmapped ATV trails. That girl, Rachel—she liked the drive. She wouldn't admit it, though Arnett could tell. She's safe from all harm now. He puts his own twist on a classic country tune he remembers Jones singing: "Her mama said, 'No, she's my only daughter,' but she got buried on the Tennessee border." Jones couldn't ever make up a line like that. Maybe Arnett should go into the entertainment business and show everybody how it's done.

About a mile ahead on the left is the access road that comes up behind Nitro, right near where he buried Leon. It runs close enough to the Lookout.

Yellow tape and traffic cones block the entrance to the access but Arnett blasts straight through, exploding the cones in all directions into the woods, tape streaming from the grille and rooftop running lights as he rattles over roots and splashes through potholes.

At the switchback where the access turns downhill again, he continues straight up until trees stop him. He parks amid soft rain and walks to the top of the mountain into his own back-yard. Wet and shivering, he goes to the shed for a jar. He flicks his lighter and finds a translucent blue Ball on the highest shelf, nearly out of reach. There it is, Jack's personal stash. A good ten years old. Jack must've used a stepladder to get up so high. Arnett never planned to drink it until the day he met the man again and kicked his ass. But tonight'll have to do. It'll be smoother and stronger than that other splo. He grabs hold, then turns it to the side to judge how much is in there. Mostly full. Enough to do the trick.

The moonshine burns open inside him like a flame and thaws his shoulders. That rain's really cold. Or it's just him—he can't quit shaking. Whichever, this'll help. Another tug and he starts thinking about the new life in front of him. Two choices, neither one of them any good. But it's better than nothing. You could sit here quiet, wait for somebody to show and then figure things out. Turner, probably. Or you could keep to your principles. Drink more. Yes. Go find what's-his-name, the dude who fucked my girlfriend who tried to kill me—Jones. Jonesy. Jonesin' for Jones. That's what we need to do. We need to go find Jones. It's all coming together now. Also, wouldn't hurt to go see Old Bob, borrow his car and do some cash collecting.

He carries the jar over to Jack's fender-rusted Cutlass resting in the side yard in a dark upgrowth of grass. Arnett had it run-ning a few times this year for business purposes. Rachel rode in it once. Inside the car with the door shut, the sound of rain on the metal roof. Drink again, it's starting to work. Now, where's the keys? They used to be right in the ignition here. Where'd he hide them? He feels under the visor, under the seat. Flips on the ceiling light, and it glows over fast-food wrappers and empty Pall Mall packs. At least the battery's not dead. Then he checks underneath the floor mat. Boom time. The largest of the keys fits into the ignition, and the engine catches and fails. Never did start the first go-round. He pumps the gas when he finally hears it cough. Okay, this shit is working.

He swallows more of the clear corn fire, takes the handkerchief from his pocket and wipes his eyes.

He follows the front access down to 231, then hits the back roads quick as possible. A few small streets with no names, just numbers—651, 238, 119. Every now and then a cluster of trailers pops up. Both low beams are gone so he's got to use the brights, and surely the tags have expired. The gas gauge shows a solid quarter tank. The oil light's a sick, feeble orange. Be lucky not to throw a rod in this sucker. And speaking of that, he should've fucked Jennifer before he left her there, then poked her again in her bleeding bullet hole.

He's drunk as fuck and starts wondering if he missed a turn. He climbs a hill, drinks more, leaves the jar open between his legs. A familiar sycamore appears, giant and sprawling, marking the right-angle turn he's made so many times. Close now. He turns off the headlights and slows down. It's dark as hell out and the jar's almost gone. He turns his head sideways and keeps one eye open, following the lines on the road. Better not fuck this up. Keep straight, goddamn it, keep *straight*.

He pulls off onto the shoulder, just a little short of Misty's. The grass is up to the car's windows, but he can see that all the lights are off. Shouldn't there be a band playing tonight? For all the bluegrass shitheads? But it looks closed. Bob's car isn't even here, just somebody's Impala. Doesn't he recognize that from somewhere? Just getting paranoid from the buzzy buzz. Better walk over close, see who's around.

He keeps the car running—might not start again—gets out, leaving the door open, and wades through the grass and up the slope of the ditch, all this grass and gravel and shit. Plus it's night-time as fuck out here. He slips and things go out. He wakes up on his head and now can't tell which way he needs to go. Finally he crawls up the ditch and into the side lot. He tries standing again but the ground slants under his feet and sends him reeling. He goes back and forth cross-legged until he finds the wall and leans his face against it.

There's a window and through it he can see a guy at the bar. Could that be Jones? Fuck yeah—it's somebody. He slides back down the ditch. The car's still running. He finds the open door and climbs in. Night wind rocks the car and sends more rain against the roof. The wavering lights of a vehicle appear over an invisible hill in the distance at what seems to be a crawl. They get closer and turn into a tan Bronco roaring by him in a rush of spray, splashing his car in passing, its red taillights then rising and falling and jerking with dips in the road before disappearing. Did they even notice him? Probably not. Just another junker in the grass.

He goes back to watching Misty's. Nobody's in the Impala. And whoever's in the bar hasn't come out yet. Where the hell's Bob at? Arnett's never seen the place closed this early. Maybe Jones started singing and everybody just said, Fuck it, we outta here.

Arnett hates the concept of singing, though if he had to do it he'd definitely be better than Jones. Motherfucker couldn't buy talent if it was on sale at Wal-Mart.

Somebody else's bound to show up, though, looking for some hooch and poontwang. And somebody does, that raised Bronco, coming back from wherever it went, pulling into the lot with its headlights sweeping across the lone car. The antennas are suspicious and it looks like there might be cop lights inside against the windshield not yet turned on. It stops at the entrance and two staties get out. Goddamn, that's that same trooper truck. There's a static burst of a walkie-talkie. The man in front speaks into his shoulder.

※◇※

Turner's got his phone on the bar in front of him, next to a bunch of empty Bud bottles standing like poorly set bowling pins, when he sees headlights outside. He's got a strike.

He looks out the rain-flecked window and, what the shit—his old colleagues? He better be standing up when they walk in. Show them he's in control of the situation, not sitting around on the damn job. He lifts himself off the barstool and hikes up his pants. The Bronco's still idling, and Deputy Derek and Sheriff Ricky—who could believe it?—get out in white cowboy hats.

Here we go.

Turner walks behind the bar. Be cool. Don't get excited. But he can already feel those hives burning his balls.

Ricky pulls open the door, a clipped mustache and straightened teeth. When he first joined the force, he had braces. Turner taught him a lot. He had even arrested Ricky's brother Ray a couple times, first for fighting, then for running off during a work-release program from jail. Ray was a beast, no possibility of rehabilitation. That was what had turned Ricky on to getting into law enforcement from the get-go. His braces eventually came off and that little faggot turned into one of the toughest cops around. And now here was this situation.

Derek's standing behind Ricky with his hand at his baton.

Ricky nods at Turner. "Thought that was your car out there."

"You *still* thinking that? Then you sure are sharp."

"Don't start barking," Derek says.

"Who are you waiting on?" Ricky says.

"What makes you think I'm waiting?"

Derek steps up to Ricky's side. "I'm telling you, man."

"Derek," Ricky says, "show some respect. Turner's no longer with us on the force, but I have the suspicion he might know a few things we don't. Concerning this guy, Arnett, and the boy he killed. Leon, I believe? Might I be correct in any of this?"

"You talked to Larry," Turner says. "So you already know."

"I talked to Larry, yes. I believe he's still a little bent out of shape by how he and you were dealt with."

"Fired, you mean."

"Why don't you let it go," Derek says.

"Larry's wife called us," Ricky says, "and she told us to check on the Hickory. We did that. Folks there said they'd just driven over from Misty's because you showed up and made everybody leave. Which seems to be the case." He looks around the empty room. Knocked-over chairs, half-drunk beers. A couple jackets. Even somebody's purse.

"I don't know about much of that," Turner says.

"What else don't you know? Be honest and clear. If you lie or withhold information, you *will* go to jail. This is me helping you. Now, why are you here?"

"Because you missed Arnett," he says. "I was watching."

"Yeah. From South Mountain. We saw you. So he came back after we left?"

"He was on the roof the whole time and he just went walking off on foot."

"Where was he going?"

Turner points at the little notepad Derek's scribbling in. "You know, if you spent half as much time looking around as you do practicing your ABCs . . ."

"It's just so I don't have to look at you."

"Ooo, whoa, yeah," Turner says. "There it is."

"Where was he going?" Ricky says to Turner. "What direction?"

"Are you trying to get me in trouble?"

"I promise you," Ricky says, "you're the last person in the world I care about right now."

"That gives me hurt feelings," Turner says.

Derek laughs, then stops when Ricky cocks his head at him. "Where was he going?"

"Like I say, he was walking. Could either be somewhere along 231, or anywhere on the back access. Or East Ridge. Might as well check Buzzard Hollow while you're at it. And how about Kentucky, too?"

"All right," Ricky says. "So if you have no assumptions about Arnett's whereabouts, why are you sitting in this bar with the lights out?"

"Thinking," Turner says.

"There's a lie," Derek says.

✕◈✕

Through the rain-spattered windshield, Arnett watches the cops leave Misty's, get into their Bronco and pull out, the tires peeling and yipping over the wet road.

"About fucking *time*," Arnett says. "Daddy go get drinky. Go listen to somebody whining about somebody with no love in their life. Daddy's thirsty."

He steps out of the car holding the fiddle case and moves through the tall wet grass without hurry. He decides not to be drunk anymore and only trips a couple times. Rain's just an idea he can take or leave. He walks through the waterfall coming off the roof and slides into Misty's like the old days when he was just a drinker getting into innocent crimes, and later when he worked here for a year. He's too drunk to be surprised when he sees Turner standing behind the bar, his back to the door, taking something off the top shelf.

"I thought y'all left already." Turner begins pouring himself a drink. "I told you everything I know about that murdering son of a bitch."

Arnett takes a seat at a booth and opens his fiddle case. "What'd you just call my momma?"

Turner looks around.

"So them bastards're after me because of you?"

"I didn't say bull to them."

"Now you can say it to me."

"What do you want, Arnie?"

"Let's start right there. Don't call me that fucking name again. How about some respect. Got any of that? Go ahead. Call me that fucking name again." He's definitely still drunk—can almost see two Turners—but feels a lot clearer than he did a minute ago. He'll shoot Turner. Both of hims. He will do that. That's what's about to happen. "Now where's this guy Jones at?"

Turner looks at the open fiddle case with Arnett's hands inside. "You got a gun in that thing there, I bet."

"Why ain't you pouring me a cold one?" Arnett says. "How long must Daddy gotta wait for?"

Turner grabs a pint glass from the rack.

Arnett aims the pistol and pulls the trigger. A bottle bursts and liquor pours down the shelves as Turner drops down below. Arnett gets up and trips as he fires again and a piece of the bar opens in a disaster of splinters.

"Officer down, officer down!" Turner yells. "We got a predicament. Send in backup."

"Where'd I hit you at?" Arnett says. He falls back on the bench, gun now in both hands, and sweeps the barrel back and forth, aiming at bottles like at a carnival shooting gallery. But then, strange as hell, something comes whistling at him through the shattered bar board. He feels the speed of it grazing past and then there's a bolt stuck next to him in the bench he's sitting on.

"Fucking what, motherfucker?" Arnett finds himself moving toward the bar, unsure of what all the noise is about, until he realizes he's discharging bullets in Turner's general direction. Splinters of wood popping, bottles exploding. He's still pulling the trigger, the chamber turning and the hammer clicking, after the last bullet's spent. He steps around the bar and there's Turner with blood soaking his pants.

"Almost got me," Arnett tells him. "With that damn thing there. How'd you *do* that?"

"You. You sick son of a bitch." Turner's holding on to his leg. "And, and I know what you done and . . ." He spits through his teeth. "And where you done it. And." His face closes up in pain. "You're under arrest. Police. Me."

A crossbow lies on the floor against the cooler. "That the only arrow comes with it?" Arnett picks it up, checks it out, brings it back to where he was sitting and yanks the bolt out of the bench and tries to figure how to load it.

"Those troopers're bound to be back any minute now," Turner says.

"You say that like you're praying."

"They'll be back."

"Then I don't got time to fool with this." He sets the crossbow down, goes to Turner and shoves the pistol barrel into Turner's mouth, metal scraping against teeth. Turner cries out and Arnett pulls the trigger. The hammer clicks. Turner squeals a denial of his false fate and Arnett tosses the gun into the drain bucket by the taps where it splashes and disappears beneath the foamy muck.

He grabs a thick roll of duct tape from the top of the cooler, kicks some sense out of Turner's head, clamps his hands over his mouth, runs the tape around the back of his head, over and under his wrists and around the back of his head again and again. Then he tapes Turner's ankles together and staggers out the door.

Around the side of the building he unfastens the green hose from the spigot and pulls it over to the fuel oil tank, unscrews the cap and drops one end of the hose in until he feels it go slack from touching bottom. He unreels it alongside him as he shuffles back in through the side door.

He sucks and sucks on the end of the hose until the siphon finally works and he spits out the sour oil. The hose continues pissing onto the floor, filling the place with fumes. Turner's tape-muted shouts from behind the bar remind Arnett he almost forgot something. He steps over Turner and grabs a bottle for the road. Some beers for hydration. Keep this shit fucking going. The oil is pooling and mixing with blood. Turner kicks at his feet but Arnett stomps him and sends him into a distorted howl. The fumes are making it hard to breathe. Pretty good buzz. Fuck yeah. Arnett picks the crossbow up and gets his lighter out.

※◇※

Flames rise and lap in succession. Tall tongues of fire. Black smoke billows and hides the stars.

Three county elders have gathered, standing back from the blaze in solemn speculation. Their thin silhouettes bend and wave in the heat and light.

"Somebody call the cops," says Elvin.

"We already done that," says Bill. He's the one who started this Senior Citizen Security Force. He got out of bed to rush over here, and his sweatsuit's wrinkled. He taps a Maglite against his thigh and makes it come back on.

Elvin takes the cigarette from his mouth and points with it. "I seen his car driving that a way, boys, north toward 231 there."

"Nah, he went there a way," says Rob, pointing in the opposite direction. He's sipping from a steaming mug that smells of instant coffee and Old Crow.

"He didn't drive nowhere," says Bill. "His car's still here. Right there." He points. "That's Turner's car. I bet he done it, crazy rat bastard."

They all step back as a section of tiled roof melts and collapses and the front of the building blooms.

"Jesus drinking a Bloody Mary," says Elvin.

"Find a dimmer bulb than Turner," says Bill, "and the whole world'll go dark. You want to burn down a bar, you oughtn't go leaving your car there."

Rob drops his light. "Wait, y'all. Is that him there?"

And yes, it is.

Turner's crawling from somewhere behind the building, elbowing and kneeing and grub-worming toward them, cursing through his hands taped over his mouth.

✹◈✹

Sharon and Larry, beneath the blankets. Just voice, breath, touch. Let the rest of the world fall away.

When the phone rings, she whispers, "Don't get it."

"I'll be right back."

"Just for once? It'll stop."

She used to make him come so hard from a blow job that his feet would rattle the end of the bed. She plans on that now.

The phone starts ringing again.

He leaves the bedroom door open and the light from the hallway hurts her eyes. She brings the sheet up to her nose, smells the detergent in its fabric, then pulls it over her face and turns the light into a glow. She smoothes her hand down her belly and listens.

She can't make out what he's saying in there, but she pretends it's another woman. Back when they got together, he used to say all kinds of nasty things, even talk about other women when she let him. At first it embarrassed her. But when they were alone, in bed in the dark, she was okay with that talk. Sometimes she asked him to. Just don't go around thinking it's for real, she told him. And then he stopped for good when he admitted it was making him want others. But right now she misses those words. Those women. Even if they were names they both knew.

He's talking to one of them now. Telling her now's a good time to come over. Wife's in bed, ready to go. I'm waiting for you both, Sharon thinks, and dips her middle and ring finger inside herself.

His voice stops and she hears his footsteps in the hallway, heavier than usual. The weight of bad news. He walks across their room to the closet and gets his rain jacket. "That was Kevin," he says. "Durty Misty's is on fire."

"You're driving all the way over there in this rain?"

"Turner's asking for me. They've got him in an ambulance. Sounds like he's in bad shape. And the cops are questioning him."

"Don't go."

"I got to."

She sits there on the side of the bed, listening to his car roll down their driveway and accelerate into the night. He better be careful going over that mountain. He knows damn well he doesn't always have to get involved. She pushes her toes into the thick carpet, traces the stretch marks on her breast with a bitten fingernail. Then she does something she's never done before. She gets down and prays, naked.

XOX

A rnett knows you can't do over what you've already done. He knows that. And if you try to, that's you going back on yourself and still not fixing shit. Like any of it could be fixed anyway. It's all fucked up and you can't unfuck it up, shouldn't even think about it. That's you putting everything that makes you who you are in the dump, and then what are you? Nothing. Absolutely fucking nothing left of you, except for the trouble you started, and then you can't even stand behind that and say, That's right, I done that. I stood up for myself. No, you got to have something to live by. Some people have religion, family— shit like that. You got you and what you done. So say it with me: I am not sorry.

But he is, he is. What he did to Jennifer. That's a large dull thing in the middle of his chest fucking with his breathing.

There's also the other stuff he did, but don't think about that right now—you didn't do it. That's what you got to believe to make it through this. You didn't do a goddamn thing. Why would he have? He had no reason to.

He reaches around on the floor. The full bottle of whiskey he took from Misty's, a fifth of something fancy, is clicking between some beer cans. He picks it up, closes his knees around it, pulls the cork and tosses it out the window. He lifts the kisser to his mouth and listens to the whiskey making its exit music, glugging lower in pitch with every gulp. Din, don, down, done. "Apple juice," he says. "What if one time Daddy got thirsty and there ain't no more apple juice? What does he do then? Must he go into town? Why must Daddy do these things?"

He backhands his lips. Goddamn this shit's good. Why did anybody ever keep coming to buy his daddy's corn with stuff like this around? Why risk law and decency when you could drive somewhere and steal a bottle like this one right here? The world is a cage full of starving animals that don't realize they can just push the door open. So let's push it open.

He rounds a curve and a mashed-up buck lying in the road comes into the headlights. He has no time to swerve—good thing too, else he'd have thrown his ass off the road—and it thumps beneath him. He drives on with the sound of dragging and the smell of burning meat wafting from the vents.

He stops there in the middle of this county highway on a plateau overlooking blackness. The noise of crickets and cicadas. The car's brights bring out the dead gray of maples and oaks and poplars and telephone poles covered in kudzu and the road ahead of him and the steam rising up off the car's grille. When he gets out, he sees a five-point antler and a duffel bag-size body, what used to be a body, now just twisted fur and muscles and a stomach split open and spilling chewed grass. He grabs into the neck. His fingers go deep, it's still warm in there, fresh dead, and he slides them back out to inspect the color in the headlights and then wipes around his eyes, painting himself like Bob used to do when they went out. A buck-blood warrior.

The only thing watching him is a barred owl up in a treetop. He doesn't see it, just hears its call. He listens, considering its question: *Who cooks for you? Who cooks for you?*

He tears free a piece of flesh, puts it in his mouth and chews. It makes his stomach clench and growl. *I cook for me.*

He speeds off drinking whiskey to wash down the meat. He could jump a fence right now. With the buck's blood around his eyes, he can see things nobody else can or ever has.

The marble eyes of a baby coon flash in the left lane and he crosses the center line to try and hit it, and then the car's rocking and bouncing and a tree crashes into the left side and a ditch of shale and leaves and weeds jumps up at him and throws the car in the air, and he sees the ridge and sky and valley and a life of endless mistakes and stupid ideas on how to make money and then somehow the car lands evenly on all four wheels, right back in the middle of the road.

The engine's still running. Which direction was he going? He would never do anything without a reason to do it. The rearview broke off. He turns and looks for what sounds like footsteps— some stranger coming up on him to see what happened? But it's just his heart. Shit. He reaches down and finds the bottle. It spilled some. Double shit. The left headlight's out and the other one's bent crooked so it looks to him like he's constantly turning, but he's not even moving. He takes a hot splash down his throat to stay clear. She tried to kill him. He should've shot her dead. Left her like that and saved everybody the trouble. She tried to kill him. But he loves her and he could never do that to her, not her, can't even believe what he already did. She even bailed him out when he got spanked with that voyeurism bullshit. He still has yet to be convicted there. Free till then, motherfuckers. Let's make the most of this. He's not hiding anything. There are reasons for what Daddy does. He had a camera in the bathroom. So . . . fucking . . . what? There's bigger problems now.

The bottle's gone. He tosses it somewhere. He needs to get back to Jennifer and make sure she's cool.

�◇ж

Locked in under double-shoulder seat belts, Ricky and Derek jolt on the Bronco's front bench. They're both chewing dip, spitting into the same paper cup.

When they left Misty's the first time, it was just old Turner in there. They drove ten miles down 231, then turned around and saw the sky glowing. They came tearing back into the lot and found Turner lying there surrounded by a trio of old-timers. One was pouring something from a mug onto Turner's duct-taped mouth and hands while the other pushed at the tape with the rubber end of his cane. "I don't want to touch him," he said.

Ricky bent down and stripped off the tape. "Almost got him!" Turner gasped through his lips. Then Ricky's radio crackled. Arnett was seen driving out of town, not toward the Lookout but heading back on 15 toward Buzzard Hollow Road.

So that's the direction the troopers are rolling now, across the valley and into the mountains. It's stopped raining but the clouds haven't cleared.

"Gets dark out here, huh?" Derek says, cutting the wheel left and leaning into the long turn that begins the steep incline.

"Dangerous too, this fast."

"You want me to slow down?"

"No. Just don't jerk the wheel again."

They move through Green Hollow, past the lights of the Shif-flett house and on up through this natural disaster of trees and rocks and hills too steep for any four-legged creature to climb. Even a problem for vehicles on the road. Derek makes another hard turn and Ricky's about to say something when they see a headlight.

"That a motorcycle?" Derek says.

"Slow down," Ricky says. "Give your brights."

Derek flips the switch and the embankments on either side spring up into cliffs of clay and shale. Up ahead there's a car trying to turn around in the middle of the road, with a buck's bloody head hanging from the grille and a mess of meat dragging beneath. It comes on at a slow speed now and directly into their lights, which are bright enough to show who's driving.

They stop a moment to witness the face of Arnett in the steam, blood smeared all around his eyes and a trail of vomit from his mouth down his chest. As he passes he flicks a cigarette into the Bronco's open window, right onto Derek's lap. Derek smacks it out in short showers of sparks and then they're on the shoulder, trying to turn around while Arnett speeds off.

"Should I have blocked him?" Derek says, getting up to speed.

"Probably. I wouldn't have, though. See if we can't catch up and persuade him off the road."

※◇※

Anything's better than jail. The hollow hallucinatory echoing through the tiled hallways and off the metal-and-concrete cells. The empty sound of doors opening and closing. And the people. Around when Jack ran away, Arnett went in on drunk charges and had this guy named Ray for a cellmate. Ray had one glass eye that made him look confused. Arnett was just twenty when he walked into that cell and saw Ray sitting on the top bunk with his hands inside his jumper.

I lost my eye in a fight, Ray said.

And though Arnett didn't doubt him, he said, Who the fuck asked?

I like to fuck, Ray said.

The guard told Ray to get his hands out of there, then locked the door and went away.

The metal cot hanging from the wall beneath Ray's roost gave Arnett a place to lie down. He woke from a sleep he hadn't had in a long time with Ray shaking his shoulder.

I got a question, he whispered in the dark. You wanna be Mommy or Daddy?

Who the fuck are you? Arnett said.

Ray brought out a toothbrush of melted and sharpened plastic and sliced into Arnett's cheek, releasing the warmth of fresh blood.

Arnett saw that Ray's face had pores the size of needle holes. The glass eye was looking at the ceiling.

I ain't got to answer a single one of your fucking questions, Arnett told him.

But you will.

When the man showed him the toothbrush again, Arnett sat up and pressed back against those cold painted cinderbricks and said, Okay, okay. The two men sat there like overgrown boys playing a bunk-bed game of house. On the flat foam mattress that softened nothing, Arnett's hands were shaking. I'll be Daddy, he said.

Ray leaned toward him, grinned and said, Come here and suck Mommy's dick.

Arnett ain't going back this time.

He tells himself it's not them behind him until he can't anymore. That fucking Bronco's right up his ass. Then the brightest damn lights hit him from behind and the pull-over lights are strobing and spinning and he can't see a goddamn thing for all the steam in front of him and the wall of brightness behind him. What are they trying to do, make this situation more dangerous? Better not think of anything right now besides finding Jennifer and making sure she's all right. Make sure she drank her water. Got to keep going straight. Don't slow down. They'll stop you if you slow down, and then what are you? A cell rat again. Mommy's daddy.

A full beer can under the gas pedal keeps getting in his way. Where'd that come from? Must've been thinking ahead somewhere back there. He lets his foot off, rolls the can toward him and takes it up. The car won't go straight, or maybe it's just him. He brakes for a banked turn ahead and sees faces up in the tree branches, Leon wearing a mask of himself, breath smoking through the mouth hole, Leon lying there on the ground with his arms out flat, Leon flying crookedly like some ungainly bat, Leon staring past everything and trying to understand the dent in his head.

Arnett wipes his eyes and sees his mother in the barn stall, held to the cedar posts by ratchet straps. Deer leg hanging out of her like it was her third leg. Jack buried her in the ridge and Arnett watched him from the woods. Goddamn it. Jack came up to him with the leg. Bend over, son a mine. More weeping than he's used to these days but he can't help it. When he brakes again and looks behind him and sees the Bronco right there, it's hard to believe any of this.

The Bronco rams him and sends him skidding. He pounds his brakes and they hit him again. He lets go of the wheel, takes the crossbow from the passenger seat and holds it out his window. A shotgun blast shatters glass and sprays the back of his head with buckshot. He recovers from the reeling and steps on the gas, straddling the double yellow with the back of his neck burning. He can see the sky, full of holes, the violent stars, the guardrail, the moon a big puncture wound.

Upside down. The smell of earth and leaves. Peaceful.

He's lying on the ceiling like a baby.

Everything's everywhere.

Spots on his neck feel like flames when he touches them. Take care of them. Cover them.

People in the leaves above him now, cops coming down. He can't stop laughing. He's bleeding. He's in a gully, the solid, skinned tree trunks holding the car like an enormous skeleton hand reaching up from a lower world and gripping. Then there's a flashlight, voices. They're calling for him, asking if he can hear them. Light finds his face. Shoot me, motherfuckers. End this shit. He closes his eyes against the bright beams and voices are yelling to him and he's still laughing, and then a dark hole opens up that he can look through and see everything else surrounding it, no more shouts now, only laughter, and his fingertips just can't keep any of this inside him anymore.

XOX

ones is on the road with a full tank and a red Solo cup between his legs full of coffee from the hobo camp. Bulldozed hills on either side of the highway as he passes beneath I-81, the river of noise and metal.

Two hours out of Ashland and his cell phone just went dead. No idea where that damn cigarette-lighter plug-in charger's at. Probably accidentally threw it away at the gas station while he was trying to clean things out in here.

Holding to the limit in the right lane, he leans over, pops open the glove box and takes out the state road map with phone numbers scrawled in the margins. He used to have all these memorized, before he got a cell. He glances every other second from the map to the road to the map. He hits a pothole and hot coffee spills into his crotch. He swerves as he tries to scoot back from the warmth that's already soaking through his fly. At least it doesn't burn. And when he looks back at the map, there's what he was hoping for, the Hickory's phone number. He needs to check on how Larry's doing.

Signs for Bordon begin popping up and he stops at a gas station's pay phone.

On the third ring, a lady answers and tells him Larry's taking the next couple days off.

"Now, who's this?"

"Tiff."

"Hey, girl. It's Jones. How you doing? Y'all got anybody playing tonight?"

"Yeah, the Jaguars."

"Right on. Can I get an opening slot? I'll take tips. A beer. A floor to crash on. Or nothing."

"Jones," she says. "Of course, there's always a slot for you. That's what slots are for."

"Thanks for that, Tiff."

"You show up at six and we can squeak you in."

Bless Tiff, man. This isn't the first time she's hooked him up with a walk-in appointment. Problem now will be avoiding her after-hours special.

Now he's got a couple hours to kill. The day's been good so far. Since he left the camp it's been nothing but the hum of road noise with the sun angled and strong, turning the mountains purple and orange. Behind him it looks like an evening thunderstorm. He tried the radio once and found only a classic-rock station doing an Eagles marathon. That one line, *Don't let the sound of your own wheels drive you crazy.* How could the sound of wheels ever make anybody crazy? What'll drive you crazy is the sound of wheels *not* rolling.

When he finally pulls into the Hickory's lot, half his ass is asleep and cramped. He gets out and kicks the air. A lot more cars here than usual, even for the Jaguars. There's Kit's green Geo, and Chris's blue work truck's hidden in the far corner to avoid being spotted by enemies—wife, boss, kids. Thunder rumbles beyond the mountains to the east over in Bordon. He leaves his van right there in plain sight since he's not hiding. The setting sun's lighting up the thunderheads and everything's got that sugared look to it.

Inside, cigarette smoke hangs above the bar and Kit's in the back throwing darts. Chris is lounging by himself at a table, waiting for the music. He doesn't really care for the rest of the crowd. Tiff's got heavy metal blasting so loud over the sound system that Jones doesn't even notice who he's walking past until somebody yells his name.

He turns around and there's Shane and Tiny Tina. Shane's sitting on the barstool with his legs crossed and Tina's strad-

dling his top knee, moving back and forth like she's on a penny-
pony ride. He knows them from Misty's. Never seen them here
before.

"Jones!" she says.

"Young!" Shane says.

"Y'all? What in the world?"

"You won't believe it. It was awesome. We're over at Misty's
and Turner comes in and starts losing his shit. Nobody knows
what he's talking about. Code red this, code red that. We're all
like, 'What the fuck's a code red?' He's swinging a crossbow
around. I'm ducking. Shane's running."

"A fucking crossbow, man!" Shane says.

"He even kicked Bob out. You should've seen it. Bob about
wrecked his car peeling outta there. He must've thought it was
another bust."

"It's true," Shane says. "Mr. T's got that place on lockdown.
There's going to be a lot of folks here tonight, between the Jaguars playing and Misty's being closed."

Sounds to Jones like shit's really going down. But hell, a
packed house? This could make him more than just gas money.
"So how's life?" he says.

"Same," Tina says, rocking her head to the metal.

"I swear," Shane says. "Give her what she wants and she still
keeps bitching."

"All I want you to give me is beer," she says. "A beer. Just one
more."

"And then another one," Shane says. "Soon as you make
some money, I will buy you one."

"You know I can't work." She holds up her hand, pulls down
her sleeve and shows Jones a gash running down her wrist.
Sutures like badly drawn railroad tracks hold the cut closed. "I'm
not even supposed to be moving right now," she says. "Living,

even. I'm supposed to be dead. Or laid flat in some hospital bed about to kick it. And he wants me to work?"

"You done it to yourself," Shane says. "Getting all depressed and shit. Get happy for once. Do that for me."

"Why don't I buy you both a beer," Jones says.

Tina's fingernails tap up and down the stitches. "My baby," she says to the gash. "I'll never let nobody hurt you or touch you."

"Jones wants to buy us a beer," Shane says.

"Two," Tina says.

"Anybody back there serving?" Jones says. "I talked with Tiff earlier. She told me to come by. They're letting me open."

"I seen some chick around doing something," Shane says.

"Jones," Chris calls. "You on tonight? Hell yeah, bud. Play that one about my ex."

"We've had this conversation, Christopher," he says. "It ain't about her."

He takes down the rest of his pint and his bottom lip comes up over his mustache, sucking beer foam from the hair. "Yes it is."

Tiff steps out from the kitchen with her mouth wide in amazement, like she's never seen this room before. She and Jones lock eyes. Her face is covered in powdery makeup—or maybe it's just that her skin is so pale when framed by her dyed-black hair. He hasn't seen her in a while. Be good to catch up. Go to the bar.

"What would you like?" she says. She doesn't quite look at him.

"Whatever's coldest."

"That'd be me," she says.

"Second coldest, then."

She opens the corner cooler. "Where you sleeping tonight?"

"Wherever. Probably in my van."

"Will y'all quit bragging about all this sleep stuff?" Tina says. "I swear, I've been awake for three years." She holds out two thumbs and a pinkie. "Look at me. I am *fabulous.*"

Tiff pops the top of a Busch and sets it in front of Jones. "You're sleeping with me tonight," she says.

"Thanks." He swigs. "But I'd like to keep my options open." He lays down two bucks. "And what's with all this heavy metal shit you got playing?"

"There's the Jones I love."

"What you also love: Larry doesn't allow smoking in here. You know that."

"This is the best crowd he's ever had," she says. "I'm doing what *I* want tonight."

"Well then, let me buy these kids something?"

"Whatever they want," she says. "Y'all want a pitcher?"

"A pitcher!" Tina cries.

"We'll take a pitcher," Jones says. "If you don't mind."

"Take a pitcher," Tina says. "It'll last longer."

Shane pours the first pint for Tina and that quiets her down. When it's gone he tries pouring her another one but she's fallen asleep, her face buried in her crossed arms on the counter. She's murmuring, her dream world made audible.

"That was easy," Shane says.

"I think it's messing with the pills I took," she says, jerking her head up.

Good and easy, man. After that nap, today had been so good and easy. The company of those friendly bums. Coffee made with water from the ground. Sometimes it's all good and easy. Nothing you can say about it but that.

Tonight was starting to feel just as good, but deep down,

deeper than where the beer can go, Jones knows it isn't. He's sitting on the same stool with Tiff across from him, the place packed and roaring, sweating bodies pulsing against him. It's crazy to see the Misty's folks in here. Larry ought to check out this scene. Or maybe not. He'd be losing his shit, trying to keep everybody in line.

The Jags are onstage tuning. Jones passed up his chance to open, thinking he saw Natalie out there in the crowd somewhere. He decided to keep his head down and concentrate on what Tiff was bringing him. Now he's kind of drunk from all that concentrating and doesn't feel up to battling this crowd. Might as well just roll with it. The Jaguars don't need an opener anyway.

The wall phone rings. Tiff's the only one working and she holds up a finger at a man calling for a draft. "You'll learn to wait." The bright light from the kitchen surrounds her silhouette as she leans in the doorframe with the phone to her head. Her fingers pull at the pocket of her jeans while she listens. The barroom is dark compared to the kitchen, and something about how she's leaning between these two realms strikes Jones as true.

He takes out the piece of paper he's been writing that new song on from his jacket pocket and unfolds it on the bar. He picks up Tiff's pen and jots down a new line: *Some folks say there's two roads to follow.* He works out some other lines after it. He looks the lyrics over and rewrites them entirely on the backside of the paper, then reads them again. Sings them silently to himself, making chord shapes with his left hand between his legs.

Looks like he's finished the thing. It's done.

Tiff comes back and touches his arm. "Listen to me," she says. "There's a fire over at Misty's."

He laughs. "What? Like, fire as in burning?"

"As in burning to the ground."

Jones backs away from her as if she'd just insulted him. He

snatches up the paper and puts it in his pocket. Whatever's happening now, don't let anybody take that song from you.

"And they think that guy Arnett's behind it. You know, that dude that used to work there?"

Jennifer had mentioned some strange business between her and him and Leon. He'd brushed it off as the usual backstabbing bullshit. At worst, somebody'd get his ass kicked. But he can tell this is different. "Is Larry all right?"

"He's fine," she says. "He's with the cops. Sounds like he was a witness to some sort of shit. He asked me if that guy Bob was here."

"I haven't seen him. If I do . . ."

"Yeah, I told him no. He also wanted to know if you were here. I said no."

"Thanks. Yeah, I don't want nothing to do with this. I didn't do nothing. And I ain't about to get questioned on it."

"I got this real bad feeling," she says. "Larry kept asking had I seen Arnett. You hear what they found today?"

"No. What?"

"That girl," she says. "The one that's been missing?"

"Okay."

"They found her car. In the parking lot of that old Wal-Mart."

"Where the bus station's at?"

"They been looking for her for months. And now there's her car. Just, there it is. Sat there without anybody noticing."

"Well, let the cops solve the damn thing," Jones says. "I'm just drinking."

People are three deep at the bar. "Who's serving in here?" somebody shouts.

"I got to get to work," she says. "Don't leave. Please. That Arnett scares the honest hell out of me. And Larry told me to make sure you was safe, if you came around."

"I ain't going anywhere."

The Jaguars. Tight denim, western wear, greased hair, busted cowboy boots. Their banner hanging crooked behind them. The singer with a beat-up sunburst hollowbody hanging from a rhinestone strap with clusters of stones missing. He bites open a bottle with a bent tooth and spits the cap into the crowd while the other musicians vamp. "Thank y'all much for taking the time," he says into the mic. "We'll start with one of our own. We hope you fuck off."

Jones likes that they're not starting things off with a cover. And right then the pedal steel slides in and the drums click them into time, the bass thumping and everybody yelling. The nice quiet Hickory transforming into dangerous Durty Misty's. He feels blessed to the bones to be here seeing it all, hearing it all, drinking it all. Everything that's going down tonight makes the music that much more real.

Each time Tiff checks on him there's a freshly frosted pint glass full of yellow beer in front of him, and what's he supposed to do, say no? He hadn't planned on drinking tonight but now the cold brew's turning warm in his stomach and this chicken-dance honky-tonking onstage isn't helping any, except it is. All the pickers are younger than Jones. Good thing he didn't do that opening set.

He keeps getting pushed against the bar by all these drunks and smokers and dancers. Larry wouldn't stand for it. But it takes him out of his head, so he doesn't have to think about Leon or Misty's or that poor girl or whatever the hell else. Shane appears out of the wall of bodies, opens his jacket and offers Jones a drink of whiskey from a collapsing plastic fifth stuffed into his sleeve.

Tiff, with her pinwheeling green eyes under those chopped black bangs, is pouring him another pitcher and telling him to turn around. When he does, Natalie's right in his face.

"Let's go." She grabs his glass from the bar and dumps it down her throat, then hooks a finger in his belt and leads him to a table where they have a good view of the stage. He leans into her ear and says, "Look at your hair." He doesn't realize until now how drunk he is.

"It's called Car-Wash Crimson," she says, fluffing it. "Don't be worrying about me, watch them boys up there."

Cool, so nothing's wrong, just friendly exes hanging out.

He studies the bassist thumping out hand patterns. He's heard about this guy. One of the original Bristol Boys. Man plucks the strings like his hands are floating. Jones shares the pitcher with Natalie until it's gone. "I'm sorry about this morning," she says. "I been feeling bad about that all day."

"Feels like yesterday to me," Jones says. "Don't worry about it."

"Eads and Terri—they bring it out in me."

"Then quit letting them stay with you."

"I know it. That's what I did after you left. I kicked them both out and locked the doors. I'm going to make some changes in my life."

"So you came out to a Jags show?"

"Changing don't mean you gotta stop living, does it?"

"You end up sleeping with those two?"

"I thought about it. But only to hurt you. That's the only thing I would've enjoyed in it. Then I realized you were gone, so it wouldn't matter to you at all."

"It does matter. I don't want to see that stuff happening to you."

Shane and Tiny Tina drop by the table, their secret bottle becomes no secret at all and Natalie's starting to grab at Jones. Well, why not? One more round. He can taste her lipstick on the mouth of the bottle and then he's draped around her middle and sweating onto her breasts. His face is numb. They're dancing. He doesn't notice much of the music anymore. She's kicking him in the shins with her boots, telling him to hold her and swing her, and Jones can smell cigarettes in her hair and her body odor. That web of freckles spreading across the bridge of her nose. Her nipples poking through when she presses into him. He puts his arms around her and she pulls his hands back up around her waist and keeps kicking him until he starts moving to his own song, away from her and out the door.

He sits down on the ground in the parking lot, pulls out his cigarettes and falls over. He lies there smoking, little bit of rain coming down.

He hears shouting, props himself up on an elbow and sees two men swinging at each other, connecting every now and then. Oh, that's nice, like the old days. It really is a beautiful thing.

Natalie's standing near the action. "Kick his ass!" she's saying. "Kick his fucking ass!" Somebody pulls her back and drags her away. There's his girl. No changing that.

Cruiser lights strobe the trees and the building and the cars in the lot. A lady cop stands over Jones. "Are you okay, sir?"

"Just sobering," he says. "I'll be fine. You wanna get married?"

"Sure, just a sec." She walks away to help make the arrest. By the time the fighting men are cuffed, they're talking like brothers. Which they might be. The cops go inside and Jones hears the music stop, the drummer giving a final crash.

Tiff comes out after a while. "Oh my God, there you are." She crouches down and peers into Jones's face. "Damn. All right, you're sloshered."

"Where'd the music go?"

"The Jags had to quit. The cops are really pissed and sent everybody home. They're asking around about Misty's and nobody's saying nothing."

People are standing around, boots and shoes kicking around in the wet gravel. Jones lies there watching everything. The cops finally leave, and Tiff says, "Come on inside, before you get soaked." She pulls him up, helps him get against the building where it's dry, wipes his face, brushes him off. "Could've burned yourself too," she says. The cigarette he's smoking falls out of his mouth and she lights one of her menthols for him.

Jones looks around at people smoking, drinking, laughing, crying, drinking, getting ready to go home. "Where's Natalie?"

"In worse shape than you, guaranteed. Long gone."

"Shit, man. I should've made sure she didn't get like that."

"She ain't your problem. Let her go. You're enough for you to worry about."

A man tries pissing into the ditch and falls face-first into his own puddle. A couple leans against a truck, entangled. It's a lonely feeling not to be the cause of this trouble. He misses coming out to parking lots after playing shows, smoking a cigarette and knowing he was to thank for all the mess. "You know that kid who used to play bass for me?" he says. "That's who I'm worried about."

"You're starting to act like Larry," Tiff says.

"That kid's missing too. Except maybe he's been found, I don't know. Larry told me he saw Arnett burying somebody on East Ridge. He told the cops all about it."

"So that's the deal," she says. "Then I guess they're sorting it out. There's nothing you can do now except be glad you ain't missing."

Yellow. That's what Jones sees right now. Streaks of sunlight on the wall. He's crashed out on Tiff's couch, cocaine still beating through his brain. She shared some with him and Shane and Tiny Tina behind the bar after the Jaguars packed up and everybody went home. One minute he'd been on his back in the parking lot, then the next Tiff was helping him inside while he was crying and carrying on about Leon, and before he knew it he was bent over behind the bar, sniffing lines across the scratched chrome of the cooler. And now here. Pain in his bones. Too tired to even give himself hell about it. Just close your eyes again and sleep it off. But he can't.

Natalie. Goddamn. Jones, who do you really love? And is it possible to make it stop?

There's a loud explosion in his sleep and he jumps awake to all the yellow gone.

"You're talking a whole lot," Tiff says.

"Was I? I was. What day is it?"

"Sunday. Sounded like you were dreaming."

"Just thinking."

"About me, I hope."

"I was fishing. Fishing with the boys and catching largemouth. They'd hit the spinner and go dancing across the water. And then something way too big was bending my rod into the water, and I couldn't let go. We were casting off Larry's old pontoon."

She kneels down next to him, eye level. "You been sleeping all day." Her hand wipes sweat off his forehead. "C'mon, I'll make you some coffee."

"It ain't but morning."

She makes a buzzer noise with her mouth. "Wrong again. I got to go into work pretty soon."

"Guess I'll be heading out, then, if I can just rest a while longer. That damn coke screwed me all up. Where the hell you get that stuff from, anyway?"

"You need to come over to the Hickory with me."

"How come?"

"You got a tab to settle up on, big boy."

"Aw, shit. Let me just pay you and you can take it over. I thought you said I didn't owe you nothing."

"You didn't, until you about drained the keg. Larry's called me five times now. Says not to let you leave without settling up."

"Jesus Christ." Jones drops a leg off the couch. "This is crazy." Even the carpet beneath his foot feels like sandpaper. "People dying and shit burning, and Larry's worried about a few beers? What do I owe him?"

"Seventy-five."

"Can't pay it. Won't."

"He knows. Says he'll let you play it off."

Blue sky through the picture window above the TV. "Did he say he'd be around?"

"No, didn't happen to."

"All right, then. Let me give you a lift over."

Driving to the Hickory, he's still rubbing the sleep and drugs out of his eyes. All that shit going down last night, and what was he doing? Getting fucked up, just like he promised himself he wouldn't. And then you went and got too fucked up to even help the man who's helped you so many times. But what should you have done? Nothing, except not get so fucked up. All right, let's play this one off.

Nothing's as sad as the sound of happy hour ending.

Jones taps the vocal mic to see if it's coming through the PA. Two black-carpeted Peavey cabinets on either side of the stage. Fifteen-inch Black Widow speakers with a horn in each. This is Larry's investment and it sounds good. The highs are clear and the bottom's low—like the water last night in his dream. He taps again. "Can you hear me in the back?" he says. "One more time, are you getting it in the rear?"

One of the two men still at the bar laughs, and Jones ducks his head to see if he can make out who it is. Light glints through the pint of amber ale in front of the man.

"Good to know I'm not the only one," Jones says.

Larry comes onto the stage wearing unironed slacks, a white shirt and a loosened tie. "Watch your mouth, Jones," he says. "Kind of place you think this is?"

"After last night, I got no idea."

"Yeah, I've been cleaning up the remains. Heard you were in unique form."

"Not that unique. It's good to see you, Larry."

"You too. Glad to have you. You heard about Misty's? Arnett must've purely lost his mind."

"That's what Tiff said. Have you heard anything about Jennifer? She okay?"

"All I know is they caught Arnett last night. Ran him right off Buzzard Hollow Road."

"And he's still alive?"

"Apparently a tree caught him. Lucky he didn't roll."

"We'd be better off if he had."

"I know that's right."

The man at the bar gives a two-fingered whistle. "Let's go! Let's hear it!"

Jones leans into the mic. "Don't make me send the bossman down after you."

Larry pats Jones on the back. "I'll let you get to it. We can talk later."

One mic is aimed at Jones's guitar, a little ahead of the sound-hole, and the other at his mouth—the other soundhole, Natalie used to say. He's still shaky from last night and hopes that doesn't translate into the music. He wants to sound good for Tiff, whatever she's worth, and for Larry, except Larry's busy. Maybe it's just his own self he's nervous about.

He plays through the form of one of his older originals, "Kudzu Vine," and the dude at the bar starts clapping.

Jones remembers the chords okay. The words, though. He hasn't played this song in probably a year. He quits playing and says, "Just checking the levels," then leans over and pulls the lyrics to the new song from his back pocket. The paper's barely holding together and he tapes it to the mic stand. He reads through the lyrics. Yes. But let's do it right.

"Could I get some water?" he says into the mic. "Water with lots of lemon. A thousand glasses, please."

When it comes, the water's just what he needed, bringing him a little closer back to the world of the living. To warm up his throat he sings a couple by Hank, an Ernest Tubb, an early Haggard, and ends with his favorite Lefty: *I can't stand to see a good man go to waste . . .*

All right. Now he's ready to go into his own stuff.

He flatpicks a lead into the new song, and this time it's more than just seeing the words on the paper; it's diving down and living in them:

If I had my way I'd leave here tomorrow
Hitch up a ride and ride on down to Mexico
But there's just one thing I gotta do
And I don't want murder on my soul

The melody slides off the strings without him thinking about it. The sound system works nice for what he's doing; you can hear the boom in his strum.

Some folks say there's two roads to follow
One leads to glory and the other down below
I tell you right now I see only one way
And if I stay here it's my grave

He leans back for another solo but doesn't take it, just chugs, and behind his rhythm, he can hear the old band.

Sometimes at night I wake up in your arms
Sometimes I feel your fingers on my skin
Every single night I wake up dreaming
Thinking where you are and who you're with

I don't want murder on my soul
I don't want murder on my soul
Just one thing I gotta do
And I don't want murder on my soul

He ends on a big chord and lets it ring out, listening to all the other instruments inside his own as the volume fades and the overtones mix.

Then the man at the bar yells, "That ain't yours, is it?"

"It is long as you like it."

More people start showing up. Behind him, the dartboard that Larry turned into a clock reads ten after eight. They're sitting around tables now, or in the corners or huddled around Tiff at the bar. Two hours to go.

The crowd keeps thickening—no thanks to his music, just the hour—and though most folks are talking over him, he knows a few out there are listening. Always will be. He rolls through half his set, playing most of his originals and a few favorite standards. He checks his watch and it's time for a break. Let's go walk around and see who's here.

He's wedging his pick between the strings when Larry steps up onto the stage. "Sounded good," he says.

"Man, I need to apologize."

"I wanted you around tonight to make sure you're okay."

He's not looking at Jones while he talks to him, and because of this Jones knows he's for real. "And you're drinking water. That's good."

Larry glances around the room and Jones can tell he's thinking of something else.

"That boy," Larry says. "Leon. That was his body up there."

There's nothing to say. It's impossible. But why does Jones feel like he knew all along? Maybe there's a song in it somewhere. But he ought to feel ashamed for even thinking like that.

"Get it done and get off," Larry says. "No more messing around. Don't take a break. You're sleeping at my place tonight."

"I still got to pay off my tab."

"Shoot, I was just joking about that."

"Tiff thought you were serious. She about dragged me over here."

He follows Larry back to his house through the open country. With the far-off houses and the smell of Hickory Lake in the air, it should be a friendly night to be out in this warm valley, but he can't stop thinking about Leon, about Arnett, about the truth of how people live around here, how such ugly shit happens in this beautiful place. This county, his home, no longer feels like home. And that makes him feel at home.

He parks in the driveway next to Larry's Chevy and gets out of the van. The heat tonight, you can taste it. Wildflowers and black pepper. Countless miles of honeysuckle and kudzu vines twisting for life and strangling each other out at the same time.

"I should've grabbed some smokes on the way," he says.

"I've got some stashed. Come on in. Let's talk about your music, what you plan on doing with yourself. How the hell you're going to get out there and out of here."

In the kitchen, Larry pours two cups of coffee and hands one to Jones. "I'm talking about that heavier, darker stuff you're playing. You know? Not them antiques you're polishing but that low muck you like. *Murder on my soul.* Get it recorded. That song's worth more than your whole demo. Is it yours?"

"No."

"Bullshit. I can tell when you're lying."

"I wrote it. But."

"But *fuck.* It's yours. Deal with it."

"Look," Jones says. "If talking about that song helps keep your mind off what's been going on around here, that's cool with me."

"I don't think it's too far removed from what's going on around here. When you write it?"

"Recently."

"Maybe last night? Because I swear, some of it really hits home."

"No, before any of this stuff happened. Least before I heard about it."

"God Lord Jesus and whoever the fuck else is up there working with him—well, this too shall pass, won't it?" He drums his fingers against the coffee mug. "It's a song that puts you in the flow. You're at that age. Hold on to it as long as you can." He opens a toolbox beneath the sink and takes out a yellow pack of American Spirits.

"I don't know if that song's good," Jones says. "I started just singing and it came out from under what I was already writing."

"That's what I'm talking about. The flow. There's an undercurrent." Larry hands him a cigarette.

He never heard Larry talk the mystical talk before, but he knew he had it in him. Deep down, Jones is excited about the song too, how it might get better as he plays it out more. Plus he's flattered to death. He keeps his face straight.

"You know, those Jaguars," Larry says, "they're about to hit the road, going places nobody goes."

"Except for me."

"Even you haven't been there. These are big places. The Blue-bird—"

"I *been* there. I *played* there."

"One song for an open mic. I remember, I got you that gig. The Jags have a featured spot. Friday night. And their label just got them a bus."

"Fuck *all* that shit. They'll be paying it off the rest of their lives. Or no, they won't, because they'll burn out broke. I'm tired of running around all over the place. Right here is where my songs come from."

"Don't give me that Woody Guthrie squaktalk."

"This's all I really know, Larry. Sure, I could go to Nashville or L.A. or New York and hustle my ass off, but I wouldn't get nothing done."

"Nashville," Larry says. "None of the others. I set up that show for the Jaguars and I'd be happy to put you on it. We got too much talent around here not to be sending it out. You're some of it. Now that the coal's gone, music's our only damn export." He turns around and looks out the kitchen window. "You like the Jags the other night?"

"I did. They're vintage."

"They're smart, too. They won't ever have to be sleeping in vans again. Guarantee you that."

"Where all they going?"

"South, mostly. That Nashville show's yours if you want it."

"No, man. No chance."

"I'm happy to put you on it. I'd love to get you out by your-self. Like you were tonight."

"I'd rather be here."

"Bars burning down, booze-dick cheating." Larry holds his

hands out like he's weighing two meaningless things. "You know what, you're right. It's a little piece of heaven around here." Larry looks at him until Jones looks down. "A boy died over this trifling bullshit. And you still like it here?"

"I'm sorry. But I do. You do too."

"Shit," Larry says. "Help yourself to more coffee and let's just go into the living room. Bring them smokes."

Larry lights the candles arranged on top of the cast-iron wood-stove, and he and Jones sit down on the leather couch.

"I like those," Jones says.

"That's Sharon's thing."

Framed LPs of local bands that Larry's booked and promoted are hung on the knotty pine walls like family photos. Jones recognizes some. Admires one or two.

Sharon comes floating halfway down the stairs in a pink tent-shaped nightgown. When she sees who else is here, she tells Larry, "Don't stay up too late."

"Be up soon."

"Er or later," she says.

She drifts back upstairs and Jones hears the bedroom door shut.

"So," he says, "old dogs can learn new tricks."

"I'm a lucky man." Larry bows his head. "First love, music," he says. "Second, that lady."

A candle pops and a line of wax draws down its side. They put their feet up on the coffee table. Jones could never stand living in a nest like this. But it's nice right now.

"You look worried," Larry says. He's sunk in the recliner section, a mug of coffee balanced on his belly.

"It's nothing."

"Jones. You couldn't have stopped any of this."

"That supposed to be good news?"

There was one time he and Leon were quiet together, a fall night after they had played at Misty's. Jones was driving him back to his parents' place when he noticed the moon. A full round ember. "Let's stop and watch it," he said.

"No matter to me," Leon said.

Jones parked the van in the middle of the road on the Turkey Chunk bridge. They got out and sat on the railing.

The moon seemed to be sending out smoke. They sat there for a long time, Jones looking up, Leon looking down.

"You're missing it all," Jones said.

"It's down there too," Leon said. And when Jones looked down into the creek the light was pulsing off the water like mercury. A creek on fire in the moonlight. It felt dangerous to be sitting above it. And it was impossible to tell what Leon was thinking.

Larry goes into the kitchen and calls to Jones to go through the records and put something on. Larry's got hundreds of LPs leaning in the same direction along a board mounted to the wall, bookended by old torpedo-shaped window weights made of solid lead. Jones takes down some records that Larry taught him with—the Stanleys, Bill Monroe, Blue Sky Boys, the Lilly Brothers, Flatt and Scruggs. He pulls black vinyl out of a Hylo Brown sleeve and studies its grooves.

"That's a good one." Larry points, sits down and dumps a few green buds into his palm from a plastic film container. "A little piece of the rain forest," he says, then mixes it with some tobacco and rolls a spliff.

Jones puts on the record and they toke up, the sticky smoke

curling into the air. Larry brings them more coffee, and Jones's mind eases into a comfortable place he knows and likes.

After "Lost to a Stranger" Larry gets up and lifts the needle. "Doesn't get better than that."

"I know it," Jones says. "I'd like to start doing that one myself."

"But that's the problem. It's been done so many times, perfected to a point of imperfection. If you polish it any more you'll wear a hole right through." Larry's stoned, on a roll. "All those songs? Antique furniture."

The weed's working on Jones too. "I hear you," he says. "But that's what I learned on. Hell, you taught me most of them."

Larry holds up his left hand. "I didn't teach you nothing. I just let you listen. You're better now than I ever was."

"Bull. I wouldn't know the first thing if it wasn't for those songs."

"Then keep playing them. Just not onstage. They can't carry you as far as you're looking to go."

"What makes you think you know how far I'm looking to go?"

"I'm not talking about you, Jones. I'm talking about your *songs.*"

"Well," he says. "Maybe you're smart."

"Listen to this one." Larry puts on a classic.

Jones nods along to Hank's guitar chuck. He likes this song, but then there's this line: *It's hard to know another's lips will kiss you, and hold you close—.* "Now see, listen, right there." Jones points. "That line. There's something wrong in it."

"Sounds good to me," Larry says, and right then Jones feels his gut drop: he's gone past the only man who believes in him, who saw him through it all and still wants to. Listen to that verse. It's good, but it's a little off. Maybe Larry can't help him with these bigger things anymore.

He waits for Larry to answer, then realizes he hasn't even asked a question. "Well," he says, taking a sip from the mug and holding it against his chest. "I think fire, when it's hot enough, lets off a kind of release. Like there's this lowness that opens." He has no idea what he's talking about.

"You need to get out of here for a little while, Jones. What're you planning to do for money?"

"I don't know. Haul trash. Sell blood."

"Tell you what. I got a basement full of junk that I'll pay you to make disappear. And then you need to get on the tour circuit."

"Me and that van can work all kinds of trash magic."

"Good, then," Larry says. "We got a plan. Shit, I'm falling asleep here. I'll see you in the morning."

When Larry goes upstairs, Jones blows the candles out and lies on the couch, his mind racing over song ideas and all the different ways you can arrange a verse. He sees Nitro Mountain through the window. Barely visible, but there. A bump in the night with a little red light at the top. He'll never get to sleep looking at that.

3

I was working the counter at Ball Breakers, making change for strangers. The weekly tournament happened twice a week and all the local sharks came out for it. And the wing specials. I was registering teams, assigning them tables and keeping track of who got beat and who went on. It was mostly boys. The winners were the worst, strutting over to ask if I saw this or that. "Could've won it with two simple draw shots but went for a kicker in the corner instead, and then a massé around the stripe—you catch that, sweet thing?"

I didn't ever answer. They wanted me to smile. Wanted to get close. Asked what brought me here. Begged me for answers. I kept quiet, staying a riddle to them.

The bartender, Amanda—she believed in me. She said I could sleep on her couch until I found my own place. She was trying to help me out by putting up posters in her windowless bathroom, inspirational pictures paired with rock 'n' roll quotes. A dolphin jumping out of the ocean: *Break On Through to the Other Side!* A kitten hanging from a tree branch: *Don't Let Me Down.*

Maybe these things worked on normal people. I had no idea.

The couch I was sleeping on was huge and soft and so comfortable; on the wall across from it there was a flag-sized flatscreen. One night I tried turning it off and her Jack Russell straight up bit me. The TV stayed on the History Channel all night long because Amanda said Kernel liked watching war documentaries.

Amanda was the only person I liked talking to, and I still

didn't say much. I was used to being the kind of girl who couldn't be by herself. Always had to have a guy there. Actually, I liked having at least two guys. One to run away from and one to run off with. But that seemed like a long time ago. I was a different person back then. I saw my new loneliness as a success. Or at least something to keep me out of trouble. But honestly, at night it was torture.

Sitting on the couch one morning, I pulled on my blue socks. My favorite pair that I promised to keep forever. I'd never told anybody about them, except for Leon. This was back in the early days before I got my truck and he was still driving me around. I don't know why I treated him like I did, other than him being sweet, which I guess is reason enough if you think about it. Let's try not to. Anyway, I told him about the socks, about Good Steve and what that man did to me. I could see it cut him. And when I saw that, I kept going deeper. Not to hurt him, just to see what he would do. He was the only one I ever told. I didn't mean to hurt him. I trusted him.

I sat there on the couch staring at the socks on my feet, thinking about everything I put everybody through. I decided to wear them to work that night for a tournament.

A guy my age came to the register I was working and asked if I saw him out there. "Lost bad," he said. Old country music cried over the house system, a nice change from satellite radio, which was mostly rap and loud-ass rock. I opened my hands to him, showing I had nothing to offer.

But I liked his broad shoulders and clean-shaved face. Low hairline above a packed brow. He was even cuter walking away. I checked him out from behind, something I hadn't done in a while. Looked good in those Carhartts. He turned around and I did too, before I could tell if he'd caught me. The blood in my cheeks meant I was still alive.

My last boyfriend almost killed me, after I tried to get him killed. I didn't know at the time he'd already killed the guy I was with before him. And that first guy also tried to kill him. I know it sounds crazy. It was. I tried to forget about it. Pretend like nothing ever happened. Start over new. Those memories need forgetting. We were young. Still are. One of us will be young forever. I wasn't saying his name out loud. Who would that help? There was no need for punishing myself anymore. I was not getting any younger. Nobody was getting any aliver. I kept my head down. You should've seen me. There I was, making change for strangers.

It got late, close to the final match, and people were rooting around the tables. The smell of cologne and carpet conditioner. The lights went down and the drinks went down and the music went up. Girls leaning in the corners, sipping frozen mixers and watching their guys whack balls. That was the first time I noticed how good it felt not to be drunk. When you're sober, everything's a sharp image contained in its own little world. And there I was, contained in mine.

I looked around for that guy but he was off with some girl. She was all right, but she was no me. I should've let it go but I couldn't. I wanted to mess with him some. Just something small. The two of them were sitting at a table holding hands. I made more change and tallied up another team's win.

Hands on my shoulders pulled me backward. I felt Arnett dragging me down, but the hands spun me around and I saw it wasn't him. "We having fun yet?" Don was saying.

"Don't ever do that again," I said.

"So she *does* talk!"

The music was so loud that you could only yell. It smelled like he'd been drinking whatever he had the carpets cleaned with. "Listen," he said. "The hand that feeds you? Don't bite it. Okay, babe?"

He bit his finger, shook his head, tapped my cheek with the bit finger and walked away. He was an asshole but it did feel good to get handled.

The nights ended easy. All tabs settled. No disasters in the bathroom. The billiard area was always spotless: the sharks treated it like a church. It was a fifteen-minute walk back to the apartment. Kernel liked to curl up on my pillow and watch antique planes drop bombs on people. Amanda was usually asleep when I got back. I unfolded my blanket and Kernel burrowed between my legs, not letting me move the rest of the night.

I was a hard worker. A new person with a new life, quietly waiting for what I wasn't real sure. I was just keeping out of trouble.

I filled out a piece of paper for a doctor once. It was about anxiety. The bullet had just grazed my shoulder, the spot it hit had been dealt with and sutured, and now they were dealing with my mind. The doctor read my paper and told me I had PTSD. I said, "Excuse me, but Vietnam was a long time ago and if I look that old to you then you can't even *guess* what you look like to me." I pop-sucked my middle finger and stuck it at him. "Suck a fuck," I said.

That was my last day in the hospital—they couldn't hold me any longer legally—and those were the first words I'd spoken in weeks. Even longer since I'd acted like that. It got me nervous about my old crazy coming back. Everybody calm the fuck down. That's what Leon used to say. (Damn, there's his name.) I thought that would make a great bumper sticker. I spent a few months calming the fuck down.

Being a good girl isn't easy, but when you're lying low so somebody can't find you, it works.

You'd think I'd have missed him more than I did. But I

didn't miss anybody because they all reminded me of a life I was through with, and I didn't know what else to be except thankful.

I still thought I was beautiful. Except under good lighting like in public bathrooms. I tried to keep it so you couldn't really see how busted I was. What cigarettes and booze and men's hands had done to my face. It wasn't extreme, it was just like, *Whoa,* somebody wrinkled her up and tried to smooth her out again. Which you can't do. Around the eyes and the mouth there's no going back. You can't ever unwrinkle the bag. It looked like I'd been smiling too much.

Under these pool hall lights, though, I looked good. We had the black lights going in the main room and in here the overheads were on a dimmer. At eight o'clock I got to set them the way I liked, which was low. This place used to be a Chinese restaurant. You could tell by the mural on the wall across from the counter where I stood at. It still had the characters and the dragons. Some of the images were 3-D and they moved when you moved. The eyes of some bald fat guy in robes—Buddha, I guess—watched over me wherever I went.

One of the pool tables sat under the hanging light fixture for a buffet table. You could imagine Chinese food scattered across the green felt. The cues were long chopsticks. Can you see it?

These were the things I thought about at work. One night before Don left, I asked if he might give me a job in the kitchen.

He looked at my tits and said, "Only if you give me one first."

"I want to quit thinking so much," I said.

"Nobody will notice if you just keep quiet."

"Can you put me on dishes?"

"I could, but that wouldn't be very comfortable, would it? How about a mattress?"

"I don't get it," I said, right as I realized what he was talking about. Now that I was sober, I forgot to take into account other people's drunken minds and what they thought about. "How about a prep cook?" I said. "I'm good with knives."

"If you sleep with me I'll think about it before saying no."

He ended up leaving without anybody noticing. He was on the verge of causing a situation, caught himself, and then disappeared. Like a pro.

The next day he looked like he'd recovered from the last night. I waved at him and he came to me.

"Apologies for the disproportionate amount of cheer," he said. "It was just the merriment overflowing and you happened to be close. I'd like to keep you here."

"I hope you do."

Out the front windows behind him, just for a second, it looked like Arnett running past, slatted by the blinds.

"I will," he said.

"And it's fine," I said, "your merriment overflowing and all."

"No it's not. I'm your professional boss. Are you still at Amanda's?"

"Yeah, unfortunately. I mean, she's great for helping me."

"How do you deal with that dog? I saw that thing jump once from standing still to snatching a tennis ball off her shoulder."

"Oh my God, right? I was eating a slice of pizza the other day? Dog came flying by and just snapped it out of my hand."

"I've got this thing you might be interested in."

Amanda wanted to talk with me before I moved out. About my life. About improving it. She said there were a few decisions I needed to make. Like for example, I should never have any kids. Ever. I acted like she talked me into that one. I always thought of myself as being a mother someday, but given my "life patterns" she said it was probably a good thing if I made sure this didn't happen.

I nodded while she talked.

It's hard to describe the first glimpse of the room and the bed that would be my own. I was willing to do anything to make sure it didn't go away.

"Blanket, sheet, pillow," Don said. "No dog."

It was half past ten in the morning when he showed me around this cute efficiency. He was going to collect rent after I started making enough money. Until then I could stay for free.

Almost for free, I saw, as he leaned in and put his lips on my forehead.

"Whatever," I said.

I ended up sleeping with him, except there was no sleeping. Don was older and I guess he was out to prove something with me, set a record or something. I was lying on my back, taking it like a champ and staring out the window, when a rooster crowed. "I like a good cock," I said, and I think that's what made him finally come. He pulled his angry stiff thing out of me and told me to lift up my shirt, which I did, just a little, and it spat gray suds into my belly button.

"With half her clothes still on, ladies and gentlemen!" Don said.

He thought I kept my shirt on to tease him. He hadn't seen my scars.

"You're a beauty," I said, because I wanted to have somebody, some body, to keep me company at night. But the night was long done with. I asked him to lie down next to me and he rolled on his side and brought his hand over my forehead like he was taking my temperature. I calmed the fuck down.

He got up and brought me a paper towel and apologized for being so small.

I wasn't crying but for some reason I'd gotten teary. No, I was not crying. I wiped my eyes, then my belly, and said, "That was long!"

"I'm talking dick." He blubbered his tongue between his lips. "I know it's small." He put his hands on his hips and let his belly sag. "But I make up for it in hours, right? I know this," he said, "because that is what they say."

He had a bushy mustache, like a miniature version of the push broom I used when we closed. There should be a rule about not hurting the feelings of a man with a mustache. "You're big," I said. "There's no stopping you."

He sat down next to me for that one.

Not many people knew I was smart. I could tell by how he talked to me that he thought I was pretty stupid. When I told Don he was big, it wasn't exactly true. I mean, he wasn't small small. He was normal. Normal normal. Which I liked. I didn't need some alien fathership crash-landing in my cunt every time I wanted a little romance.

I swear, if it's not big enough to give you a walking disability, men think it's useless. They want something that immobilizes you. Move. Don't move. Look at me. Don't look at me.

He thought it was a shame if it wasn't something he could bludgeon a baby seal with.

But he did leave me sore.

You should've tried talking to me. Nothing came back. Even if I liked you, which I probably did.

There were a lot of people where I worked who weren't lonely, far from it, and they were always worse off than me. Sure, they were surrounded by friends, but they weren't in control of their lives. They reminded me of me back in the day. All the stuff that comes with the territory. No thanks. I'd had enough of it. I'll take lonely any day of the week.

The man I tried to have killed wrote me from jail while I was in the hospital. My nurse brought me the letter. She wasn't supposed to, so I didn't tell anybody about it. The letter was written in this neat handwriting I never knew he had.

Just the rising and falling of his cursive script made me want to see him again. I knew the nice curling tattoos on his skin but never thought he could be as neat as them. And he was. In this unbelievable handwriting he said he was in for good. We would never see each other again. *I mean you could come see me,* he wrote, *but we won't really see each other, so I'm not putting you on my visitation list. So actually you can't come see me.* Then he asked if I couldn't just get over everything that happened—*he* had—and we could start loving and trusting each other again. He needed somebody to write with. He gave me his jail number, if I ever wanted to respond. He wasn't going anywhere.

I kept that number and the jail's address. Never wrote back to him while I was in the hospital. They wouldn't have sent it. But that day before work, in bed after Don, I started thinking about Arnett's letter and how scared he must be. Or how pissed. There was responsibility here, and it was mine. I needed to follow through with it. I wobbled Don-legged to the drugstore and bought envelopes and stamps, then asked the cashier if I could have a piece of printer paper out of his printer. "I'm trying to write my boyfriend in jail."

"That's so sweet," he said.

"Can I use your pen too?"

I didn't want to write in the store. The music. The lights.

The rough surface of the trash-can lid outside made the lines I wrote look shaky. I told Arnett I'd talked to Wesley, which I hadn't. *Thought you were only getting a few years for violations of such and such. That's what Wesley said. You were at your home defending yourself and whatnot. Out of your mind from the formaldehyde. I've seen it on the news like everybody has—kids dipping joints in the shit. Anybody on a jury will know what that does to your brain.*

A man stood in the street in my periphery. I held my hand over the paper and looked. I hadn't slept at all the night before. The guy was a mirage, whisking away like steam when a car drove through him. That's when I knew I'd better make it quick. The man was Arnett.

And what about probation? How about bail? By the way, how is your stomach feeling? I really am sorry about all that.

I stuffed it in an envelope, signed the top left with a heart dotting my *i*. I began to put my new street address below, but even though he was still locked up, I decided not to. Instead I used Ball Breakers'. Then I filled out a form at the post office that directed my mail from the pool hall to me.

At home my mailbox was nailed above my downstairs neighbor's. I checked it every day before I went to work. The day his reply arrived, I opened it standing right there in the sun. That same unbelievable handwriting. He didn't sign his name. Only his number.

From then on I got one every other day, more and more letters in the neat cursive. His message was always the same as the first: *You are the love of my life, nobody in this world understands me like you do.* Stuff like that. It gave me the creeps. But then I read it again, because it's nice to be the center of somebody's universe. Forget what I said about loneliness. It was an amazing feeling to be forgiven, to be needed.

Anyway, like he said, I owed him. I did.

We knew we'd never see each other again and that made it easier. Besides me as his queen and the problems of jail—never enough food, too cold, too hot, never dark enough at night—he didn't say much in his letters. Mostly a lot of begging me to promise I was his. I wrote back and said yes. What else did he have?

And then his letters stopped. They just stopped.

Have you ever been locked up? I was. For two days on a weak claim that I was behind some of Arnett's sex videos, which is about the only illegal thing I *didn't* do. Though I did like it, I'll admit to you. When the court-appointed lawyer proved I wasn't involved with that, they let me fly on the drug stuff.

But not without a serious talking-to from the judge, a man just a little older than me with the eyes of a wanter. "I want to not hear anything else about you," he told me. "You. You. Not even a speeding ticket. Ever again. Never be here."

That scared me right out of town, really. But I was also scared that Arnett was going to make bail before the conviction date. Crossing the state line seemed like a smart thing to do.

Letters had fallen off the bus I took, and all it said on the side was *OUND.*

The station was in small little Ashland, by the abandoned Wal-Mart building. The back of the lot was full of old buses in disrepair. Better buses idled single file between the sidewalk and the traffic cones, destination signs above their windshields. One said Kingsport.

Arnett and I used to make trips down to the Tri Cities. The Hillbilly Bermuda Triangle. We were transporting what he called

Robot, a mixture of heroin and meth, and we felt good about the dynamics of the product. We traveled a lot of it in the spring, the hillsides blushing like baby cheeks. In Bristol we stopped at what looked like a garage to load the truck with gutted pinball machines, stuffed to their limit with Robot, then headed over to Johnson City and Kingsport, making the rounds to a few different bars, dropping off the machines and making bank.

We didn't drink on those trips. Arnett said we had to stay clear. I'd get the shakes so bad, but I pushed through and we made all the deliveries. Arnett knew everybody. I just stood there behind him like a smiling statue. Some of them were the nicest folks you ever met. They gave us beds in their houses. Fed us dinners. Coffee in the morning. Kingsport was the prettiest, with its open river and safe mountains. The downtown was like a cradle. It made me feel like everything was okay. Arnett was suspicious of that feeling, but I loved it. We ate a couple times at Ball Breakers. It sounded like they were always hiring. I marked it as a place to go, if I ever had to run.

I shared the front seat of the bus with a lady who'd just got out of a shelter for broken women. She was a sweet round toy who went by the name of Diana. Bandages over her wrists and no hands. We sat together and watched the night race at us headlong. I didn't mention her hands, the lack of them, but she brought it up. Said she was washing dishes one night when her husband came behind her and fed each one, fingernails first, into the garbage disposal.

I rested a hand on her shoulder.

She kept talking like she didn't notice. "My lawyer proved my husband had sharpened the blades or whatever in advance, so it showed premeditation. But I don't think that's true. He never meditated. It was passionate."

I asked why he'd done it and she said, "He saw me touching his car in the driveway. He'd just washed it and polished it.

That's why he done it. He just couldn't get the idea out of his head of my dirty hands all over his new car. It was a new Ford Focus."

"Honey," I said, "nobody's allowed to cut off anybody's hands, not over a Focus."

"Mine you can," she said. "He worked his whole life for that car."

The bus let her off at some gas station, where not a single light was on in the parking lot. The driver asked if she had somebody coming to pick her up.

"Eventually," she said.

Ball Breakers hired me like the day I got there, which was lucky. Probably because of Amanda, who I ended up ditching. And now I was a sorry-ass country song, thinking of the used-to-bes, remembering when, etcetera. Working this register. Just the words *green grass* would get my chin going. I never saw anybody, except for all those dudes playing pool. And their frosted girlfriends. And Don, of course, who smiled at me with pieces of leftovers in his teeth that his wife—yes, of course—packed and sent to work, even though we made our own food here.

I figured Arnett had got convicted. That's why he hadn't been writing me letters.

So I was standing there making change, bound to miscalculate something every other time, when Don walked up the stairs from the billiard room swinging his big hairy arms. "Mind mopping up a mess in the ladies' room," he said, "if you're not doing anything? Thanks." He shot me in the chest with his pointer finger.

I went down and dodged between the tables and through the noise of men drinking beer and betting and laughing. Loud radio rap-country from the ceiling speakers. A guy I didn't know put a cue in front of me like an arm at a tollbooth and nodded at a guy in jeans bending over to break in front of us. The triangle exploded. One solid and one stripe fell in at the same time in opposite corners. "Choose which you want," he said to the guy who held me up. "You can have it either way."

The cue lifted and I dodged through the crowd to the closet. I filled a yellow bucket on wheels with hot water and bleach, stuck the mop in and pushed it across the floor and into the ladies' room. It wasn't so bad and could've been cleaned up in less than a smoke break, but I wanted to take my time.

Don came in while I was down on one knee and reaching the mop head back beneath the toilets, trying to get it all up.

"That's good enough," he said. Now that he was in here, I could feel my panties riding up behind and showing. "I didn't mean for you to take all night. We'll deep clean it when we close."

I pulled the mop toward me and went to stand.

"Stay," he said. "Good girl."

I did, out of hatred of him I stayed kneeling on one knee and bent over, holding the mop in my hands. He probably expected me to get up and say something sharp and walk away. But I stayed, letting him look at it, until he told me to move. He was going to feel bad for doing it when I didn't say anything back.

"Ah, Jennifer," he said. "I'm just playing with you. Come on, get up, I'm just messing around. Don't make me feel like I'm making you do things you don't want to." In the mirror, he flicked his dick through his jeans.

Why hadn't I just figured it out for myself? I called information and got connected to the Ashland County Regional Jail. A voice gave me a choice of extensions to hit and I finally guessed the right one: 5 for Records. Arnett Atkins? The lady said she'd check, came back on and said, "Left eight days ago."

"But he told me he was in there for longer," I said. "Like forever. That's what he said."

"I don't know what he told you," she said. "But he had a morning discharge on, let's look here, the fourteenth. Bail."

"Well, where'd he go? You know what he's gonna do to me?"

"I can connect you with the magistrate if you'd like to make a file."

I hung up and kept my hand over the receiver like it might lash back at me. But then I got this strange feeling of excitement. Couldn't believe I hadn't thought to call. Something so damn simple. I didn't think this was how I was going to feel. Now I could tell him about Don. But no, don't start that stuff.

He was out, that was enough. The one person who'd never judged me. The one person who'd ever forgiven me.

Back home I took a shower and got into bed. Clean skin between clean sheets. I missed my bed smelling like bodies, like sweat, like dirt, like him. My scars had mostly healed, except on my shoulder. You couldn't really tell what they were anymore. I threw off the sheets and looked down at them. They could've been anything. Birthmarks. Poison ivy. Except for that graze in my shoulder, just a shade pinker than my nipples, sewn shut like lips.

I knew he was to blame for my whole situation, and for the longest time I'd hated him. That's what had sent me going after him like I did. We were always drinking and we didn't know how to stay away from each other and keep from fighting. I'll go ahead and admit it: I was a big problem. I loved fighting. But I was past all that now.

I woke up with my face in the pillow. The morning was noisy with birds in the bushes out front. It was this big bush that Don wanted me to trim but I never got around to it. I was already slacking on my duties as a tenant.

What Arnett wrote, that he'd never see me again—I felt okay with that at the time. Maybe in normal society you're not worried every day. But when there's nothing wrong, what's the point?

I left to go to work and birds scattered out of the bush.

I'd given myself time to stop for coffee and was in no rush. The little strip of downtown started with Annie's Antiques, then Carl's Café, then Mike's Music & Pawn. Carl's wasn't so bad with the smell of fresh coffee grinding and the shiny wood floors. I took a seat at the counter. Reece was working today. He had hands that always moved toward you. He took a mug hanging from a hook with a dozen others and set it in front of me.

"To go," I said.

"It's ten cents cheaper if you stay," he said. "And we got the paper for you and everything. And *I'm* here."

"I'll pay twenty cents extra," I said. "It's to go."

Reece put the mug back like it was something he'd bought just for me and now didn't know what to do with it. He was younger than me. At the small college studying remedial stuff with plans of working in forensics. If he knew half my story he wouldn't have even been trying. I walked across the street with my steaming cup. Fog on the hillsides beyond the buildings. I noticed something in the pawnshop window, an electric bass. It looked familiar. I stopped. That beat-up headstock. But it couldn't be. Or could it?

Leon, is that you?

People come and people go.

Let him go.

———

I clocked in, cleaned up and at noon I unlocked the doors and took my spot behind the register. The lunchtime drinkers crawled in and then the early-bird losers. From now until two, beer was only a dollar and all the games were free. The sign said so. You wouldn't believe the scum this deal brought in. And then he showed up.

Him. For real.

He was keeping his head down but I recognized how that body moved, forcing itself forward. He stopped in front of my register and looked at me like he was trying to think of the best way to describe me.

"A day late and a dollar short," he said.

His head was shaved. His eyes were clear and his skin was pure. Like I'd never seen him. Like he was finally in total control.

What was I supposed to do now? Everything that happened since he'd been gone, since I left, all the things I learned about myself—the time fell away.

But some things were different. He turned his head and on the back of his neck I saw these purple and white scabby pocks. They were part of him now. Scars on him for once. I held up my hand. He was right across the counter but it felt like I was waving to somebody far away. He said he liked what I'd done with my hair. I hadn't done anything to it.

"How are you doing here right now where you stand?" he said.

I didn't answer.

"So," he said. "Sounds like things have changed." He wouldn't look away from me. "It's nice to see you, Jennifer. Jennifer, standing here while the world spins around her. I'll see you again. You'll see *me* again."

When he walked back out the door the air pressure dropped. I hoped I hadn't pissed him off.

I was breaking down my register at the end of the day when Don came by. "The door's already locked," he said. "Just close it tight when you leave so nobody gets in. Hear?"

I took my time counting.

"One more thing," he said. "I don't know who that was that stopped by, but you don't need to be hanging out with him anymore."

"Don't worry," I said, "I won't tell him anything."

I put the bills in a bank bag, zipped it up and locked it in the drawer beneath the register. Then I sat there thinking for a long time but didn't get anywhere with that.

A security light flashed on in the parking lot when I pulled the door shut behind me and pushed on it to test the lock. And when I went around the corner of the building there was Arnett, sitting in a rusty hatchback with his arm out the window and a cigarette between his fingers. He pulled his arm back into the car, raised the cigarette to his face and the tip glowed.

"Need a lift?" he said.

"No."

"You don't have a car and I do."

"I like walking."

"Let me give you a ride home in my car. You don't have one. Come on. Ain't nothing wrong with my car, is there?"

Inside it smelled like gasoline. "Spent days getting this fucker running," he said. "Still illegal as shit. But so am I." He tapped a bag sitting at the base of the stickshift. "Ain't smoked in months but I did just now. I feel like King James." He turned to me. "You're a fucking bitch."

"I'm sorry," I said. And I was. It was the truth.

His short-sleeve shirt showed a fresh tattoo of teeth and eyes moving on his arm. Just a lazily drawn sketch of a nightmare. Scar-dots had crawled over onto Daffy's face. I let him talk all the way to my place about how shitty it was being back in Kingsport. "Ain't no opportunities to be opportunistic about here," he said. "I refuse to believe you ran off to this boring-ass shithole. I'm just glad I found you. It's a sign of the covenant of our relationship."

I stepped out, thanked him for the ride and shut the door.

"Hey now, whoa there," he said. "How late you work tomorrow?"

"Late."

"How late? I need to be leaving soon. We don't have a lot of time to do this."

"Six."

"That's not late. I'll pick you up here at six and show you how not late it is."

I woke up to those same birds screaming. They only knew one song. And it said only the one thing.

I stayed in bed all day. I didn't go in to work. I let the sun go down. The window started catching the colors of the clouds. Those birds sounded no different as the dark came on.

I was now a responsible person who worked long hours, and because of this I had no clean clothes. The clean sheets were from Don. I wished he'd bought me some clothes.

I walked to the coin laundry in stained sweatpants and a wrinkled T. I didn't have enough time to do this. He would come looking in an hour.

It took longer to wash everything than I thought it would. I shouldn't have even bothered. I put it all into a dryer, went out-side and smoked. Cars drove by.

What were we supposed to do when he got here? Talk about the good old days? We didn't have any. Or about what he planned to do with the rest of his life, which would be behind bars? I was going to tell him I wouldn't be there for him. While he was locked up or once he got out, if that ever happened. I was here now, but this was the last time.

I reached into the dryer and grabbed up my hot clothes and the brass buttons on my jeans burned my forearm enough to make me drop my nice shirt, the one I wanted to wear tonight, on the floor right into a puddle leaking from one of the washers.

"God damn everything," I prayed. The first words I'd spoken all day.

Then my cell phone vibrated with a voicemail. Arnett. He'd been thinking about me. Couldn't wait to see me. He loved me. He *loved* me. He sounded buzzed and pissed. "I bet you're hav-ing trouble with your words lately," he said, "so I'll help you out. Say it with me now, say it with me."

By the time my shirt was dry for the second time, I was already late to meet him. I walked down the dark street with my clothes basket on my hip. I saw Arnett waiting on the stairs beneath the porch light. Had his back turned. Long muscles showing through his shirt. He slapped a bug into his shoulder, inspected his hand, then he turned and looked straight at me. I stepped off the pavement behind a grove of cedars. Did he see me? He was still looking in my direction. He turned away again. No, he hadn't spotted me. Thank God, because I was still in those filthy clothes. What would he think? I peeked out of the cedars and untied the drawstring of my sweatpants.

I pushed my thumb under the elastic waistband of my under-wear, which had gone a week without washing. I dropped them on the ground and peeled off my socks. Where was the blue pair? They had to be in here. I found one. But where was the other?

Bent over the basket without anything covering my bottom, I scattered clothes on the ground and kept looking. The nicest gift I ever had, now I'd lost. The one secret I promised to keep, I'd thrown away. I looked down at my thin, white legs. What was I doing out here like this? I found a clean pair of panties and put them on. I picked my jeans out of the basket and gave them a shake as I poked my head around the bush. I couldn't see Arnett but his car was still there.

You shouldn't have made him wait so long. Waiting is the worst. You deserve getting yelled at. Oh, you will, you will. I glanced again at my empty porch. I heard him say, "Peek-a-boo." Fear almost tipped me over. His voice was coming from over by the neighbors' house. I forced a foot through the leg hole and looked around. The voice came again, from another part of the yard. "I see you."

I struggled to pull up my pants but had them on backwards.

Arnett now stood beside me. "Quit crying." He rubbed the back of his neck. "I saw you run over here with that little basket of yours. I'm just here to help. Don't cover up your crying. Don't cover up anything."

"I know I'm late. But I need my sock."

He stepped in front of me, put his arms around and held my hips in his hands. Two little pears. He slid his hands into the front pockets of the jeans against my butt. "You put these things on ass-backwards. Bless your sweet little heart. What are you going to do without me? Come here." He pulled my head into his chest. "That's it. That's my girl. Shut up. There you are. Come here."

"You were watching me."

He stepped back and slapped my face. "Now, wait. I didn't do nothing wrong. You know how long I was waiting on that fucking stoop? You know what they were asking about in jail? Cops coming in and taking me into rooms, asking if I knew Rachel. But they got nothing, no DNA. They just can't find her, that's all. Come on, Jennifer, I wouldn't do something like that without a reason. I *require* reasons. You know this. Anyway, I came early as a surprise. For you. I can't *believe* this bullshit. Just like every other bitch. Making you wait. Making you feel bad. Just like every fucking one."

Then he hit me straight in the nose and I fell backward and knocked my head against the ground.

I think I said something, but I couldn't tell what it was.

The sky was clear and moonless. I felt numb and far away and dizzy, like when the hospital had me on drugs. I'd known I was going to be late. I shouldn't have been so stupid.

I tried to tell him but he said, "It's all good now. I don't got much time."

His hands were hot. He held my face in them until I looked him in the eyes. My nose was bleeding into my mouth. "I forgive you," he said. "Do you not hear me? Let's get these pants on you."

I sat up and he knelt in front of me and helped me slide them off. Then he undid his pants. "Be quiet." He took my shoulders and pushed me back down. The moss was cool. He pulled down his underwear. The spread of sky above was poked with stars. I could see straight up so high, no end to it. Somebody told me one time that space is black because nothing's up there, not even air. The sky was turning above us, the stars dropping with nothing holding anything in place.

He was hurting me and I made a noise. "What's *wrong* with you?" he said.

"My socks. What good is only one?"

"You don't need your socks," he said. "You don't need any of that shit. What you need to do is hush."

He finished inside me and rolled off. It was my fault. I made him wait. He was waiting for so long. So was I. He stood up and I opened my eyes. He was nine feet tall. He walked across the yard backward. He got into his car and it went away backward.

Close my eyes. Help me listen. There's something inside all of this. Inside of me. I can feel it. I know it. It's already growing. I make the promise to myself: You are not alone. I say it out loud.

Lee Clay Johnson grew up around Nashville, Tennessee, in a family of bluegrass musicians. He holds a BA from Bennington College and an MFA from the University of Virginia. His work has appeared in the *Oxford American, The Common, Appalachian Heritage, Salamander,* and the *Mississippi Review.* He lives in St. Louis and Charlottesville, Virginia.

A NOTE ON THE TYPE

This book was set in Apolline, a typeface created in 1993 by Jean François Porchez (born 1964), the director of the French Typofonderie type foundry. Derived from drawings of Porchez's calligraphy, Apolline is not based on any particular typeface but was designed to suggest the rhythm of handwriting. Apolline was digitized and expanded in 1995 to include intermediate weights, small capitals, and glyphs for language support, making it ideal for both text and display applications.

Composed by Scribe, Philadelphia, Pennsylvania

Printed and bound by R.R. Donnelley & Sons,
Harrisonburg, Virginia

Designed by Betty Lew